WAITING
FOR THE END
OF THE WORLD

Also by Andrew Taylor

CAROLINE MINUSCULE

WAITING
FOR THE END
OF THE WORLD

A Novel of Suspense by
ANDREW TAYLOR

DODD, MEAD & COMPANY

N E W   Y O R K

Published by Dodd, Mead & Company, Inc.
79 Madison Avenue, New York, N.Y. 10016
Distributed in Canada by
McClelland and Stewart Limited, Toronto
Manufactured in the United States of America
First Edition

First published in 1984 by Victor Gollancz Ltd., London

Library of Congress Cataloging in Publication Data

Taylor, Andrew, 1951–
Waiting for the end of the world.

I. Title.
PR6070.A79W3   1984   823'.914   84–8111
ISBN 0–396–08421–4

FOR MY PARENTS

WAITING
FOR THE END
OF THE WORLD

CHAPTER 1

"The inheritors of the earth are gonna be rats and insects." The small, dark American paused for a sip of water. "The consensus of opinion is amazing, truly amazing," he confided. "Long-range projection studies of prestigious scientific institutes. Economists. Politicians when they're telling the truth. But they're saying nothing new. The mystics have been prophesying it for centuries. From Saint John to Nostradamus. The Vedas to old Mother Shipton. The cross-cultural spread of vatic warning . . . wow, I mean, the mind, the *human* mind, like yours and mine—it's phenomenal. It knows but knows not how. Our psychic antennae are sniffing out the approach of evil. The Great Beast."

William Dougal noticed that several in the audience were peering in handbags, clearing their throats, and glancing at their neighbors. The majority of them had come to hear about physical pollution; moral pollution, accompanied by Saint John and psychic antennae, embarrassed them.

The Great Beast, Dougal thought idly, would not

be a bad name for James Hanbury. In which case, the Great Beast wasn't merely expected—he was late.

Dougal sneaked a glance at his watch: twenty minutes late. The wooden chair beneath him was rubbing against the sunburned patch on the back of his left thigh. He could think of better things to do with a sultry August evening than spend it in a long, low lecture hall with too many people and too little ventilation.

The American began to soothe his listeners with facts; he must have sensed that he was making them uneasy. He talked of a nuclear power station that was leaking radioactivity. He quoted figures that showed how agricultural technology was destroying the land it used. Hysteria flickered into his voice when he dealt with the altering composition of the atmosphere and the prodigal depletion of energy resources. He criticized the apathy politicians showed toward anything that had no direct relevance to the next election.

The clapping of the audience forced the lecturer to return to his glass of water. Dougal decided to give Hanbury ten more minutes. Perhaps he wouldn't come at all. It was necessary to examine all possibilities where Hanbury was concerned. You could take nothing on trust.

Dougal looked at his insurance policy beside him. Malcolm's arms were crossed, his eyes were closed, and his massive knees nudged the back of the seat in front of him. It was extremely reassuring that Hanbury couldn't know that Malcolm was here.

Malcolm had a great barrel of a body, hard and muscular. His head, by contrast, was small, with delicate features and a reddish sheen to his close-cropped hair, which Dougal uncharitably ascribed to henna. Three months in the Mediterranean on Malcolm's boat, the *Sally-Anne*, had completely removed his flabby prison pallor.

The lecturer moved on to the interior measurements of the Great Pyramid and their connection with the flight patterns of UFOs.

The more Dougal thought about it, the stranger it seemed. Why had Hanbury rung last night? How had he known where to find Dougal? Hanbury surely had every incentive to avoid Dougal for the rest of his life. Six months ago he had not only taken liberties with Dougal's conscience but appropriated his girl friend and his share of a small fortune in diamonds.

". . . my friends, we are already *living* the Armageddon scenario. It's here and now, though it's still got a lot of room for growth. Disaster is gently infiltrating our domestic routines. At first it's so gradual that we don't even notice. The fabric of civilization is tightly stretched and full of little holes. The holes are widening into tears and rents. The veil will be torn asunder, revealing a brightness, a white heat that will shrivel our cities and explode our irresponsible technologies. The age of Aquarius becomes the age of the jackboot. Or the age of the rat."

Dougal shivered. Rats again. He wished the lecturer would change the subject. Hanbury had said it was important to meet here. Important to whom? He had added with a chuckle that it was time for them to settle accounts. Like a fool, Dougal had fallen for Hanbury's studied ambiguity and laughed back.

3

Someone in the rows ahead lit a cigarette. The woman sitting on the lecturer's left frowned; her eyebrows made Dougal think of two black and hairy caterpillars cuddling together at the start of the mating season. A streamer of smoke, opaque and air force blue, swam sluggishly through the stale air to Dougal's quivering nostrils.

Dougal's hand twitched sympathetically but pointlessly toward his pocket. He had given up smoking yesterday, in an airplane a few miles above Europe. His reflexes were taking their time over coming into line.

". . . an alternative," proclaimed the lecturer, "is one of a closed structure of two choices . . ."

No it isn't, Dougal thought. Nothing in a world that contained James Hanbury could be that simple. And seeing Hanbury again could force him to meet Amanda. Dougal had drowned his image of Amanda in a bottle of brandy on a winter evening; he didn't want to see her ghost. In fact he had made every effort to exorcise her by all the traditional methods: he had reasoned with himself; he had numbed his mind with a program of extensive self-indulgence; he had found a number of girls on Rhodes who were looking for a fortnight's fling as part of their all-inclusive holiday package.

After the second frizzy-haired social worker from Finsbury Park, Dougal had given up and turned to celibacy. He had derived a certain amount of smug and melancholy amusement from the fact that becoming unattainable seemed to have given him a fascination for women which he had never had before. There had been Zelda, for example, the curvaceous American information scientist whose determination was so great that she almost broke down Dougal's reserve. Ironically, his virtue had been saved by Hanbury's telegram: UTMOST IMPORTANCE RETURN LONDON SOONEST COLLECT SUBSTANTIAL DIVIDEND JAMES.

It had surprised Dougal that Hanbury economized on punctuation in telegrams. But he had obeyed the summons. Six months of supporting himself and Malcolm had whittled away most of his money. They had reached the point of having to earn their food and drink by playing nightly at Yanni's Bar. Malcolm had learned to play the mandolin in prison. Dougal preferred the piano but, in its absence, could vamp comfortably along on a guitar.

But why had Hanbury failed to turn up after having gone to such trouble to arrange this unexpected rendez-vous? An unpleasant question surfaced in Dougal's mind: *was* Hanbury absent? The memory of the latter's penchant for childish but effective disguises made him survey the other people in the room. He had done so before, of course, but the necessity of doing so again presented itself to him with peremptory force, like the need to touch wood or avoid the cracks between paving stones.

There were thirty or forty people in the lecture room. Most of them were clearly too young: they were students or recent students determined to keep their pasts alive. The majority were white, despite the fact that the lecture room was attached to a public library in one of the blacker areas of London. Not even London really—one of those shapeless northern suburbs with nothing of the capital except its name and disadvantages.

Dougal studied the few older people more carefully. One was a hunchback with enormously broad shoulders and a Roman nose. He was staring at the lecturer with a patronizing expression and clutching a copy of Madame Blavatsky's *Secret Doctrine*. On the other side of Malcolm was a tiny old lady sitting bolt upright among a cluster of grubby carrier bags. She wore a gray suit and a black velvet hat, the latter held in place with a hatpin. She would have been smart if one hadn't sensed—by smell—that she had put the outfit on at some point in the 1940s and never taken it off.

No, not even Hanbury could be secreted among this audience. Dougal turned his attention to the oak table at the head of the room. The woman on the lecturer's left had long ragged hair, a long skirt, and a T-shirt that revealed rather more of the shape of her pendulous breasts than Dougal had any desire to see. She, he remembered from the beginning of the lecture, was the secretary of the society that had organized this evening. On the lecturer's right was a thin, wiry man with freckles and glasses. The president? The lecturer himself had green eyes in an olive skin. His shoulders were hunched forward and his long arms extended, as if he were trying to get as close to his audience as possible.

Nausea took Dougal unawares and the colors in front of his eyes rippled and bulged slightly, as if bobbing on a tidal swell. Sensory distortions were at least interesting, which was more than could be said of most of the other side effects of his decreasing nicotine level. He tried to take his mind off the subject by concentrat-

6

ing on the lecture, which had now reached its peroration.

"We must save ourselves. No one else will. We cannot hope to avoid disaster and desolation by pretending it's not there." The lecturer paused to take an impressively long swallow of water. The secretary swiftly refilled his glass. Dougal remembered that she had introduced him as Dr. Vertag of the Sealed Servants. *Of the Apocalypse*, Dougal thought. *Revelation.*

Perhaps Hanbury was making contingency plans for the end of the world.

"There are *no* solutions." Vertag's ears were slightly pointed; he must have fairy blood in him. "But the Sealed Servants have a positive, coordinated strategy for facing the problems. Our aim is simple: we shall survive; we shall adapt to the new, harsher environment of the post-Armageddon phase; and we shall carry something of ourselves into the future."

Dr. Vertag paused, his head cocked to one side, as if listening to the distant sound of applause. His audience stared stolidly at him.

"Well, you're thinking, it's just another freak organization run by a semireligious nut. You probably think I'm after your spare change and a slice of your souls, like everyone else on this planet. You're wrong, folks. I don't want you to join the Sealed Servants. I want to find out if we want *you*."

Dougal sensed that everyone, himself included, was leaning infinitesimally closer to Vertag. Up to now, the lecture had been a predictable rehash of gloomy prognostications culled from the fashionable interests of today and yesterday: the occult, environmentalism,

7

no nukism, and political pessimism. Vertag wasn't appealing to his hearers' minds; he was playing on their fear of the dark.

But now he had changed his tactics and begun to apply shrewd commercial psychology: make people think they can't have something and they will invariably want it.

"Many are called, I guess, but few are chosen. If you're interested, take a leaflet. If you're still interested when you've read it, contact the address it gives with the information we ask for. Each application is processed by a panel of experts and then doublescanned by our computer. We even analyze your handwriting. Then, if *we're* interested—that is, if you're in the lucky ten percent who get that far—we'll approach you for a program of tests and interviews. We don't want maybes or fainthearts or ego trippers or passengers, okay? We need dedicated, self-sufficient people who want to stay living and are prepared to do something about it. You don't have to be religious, though some of us are, but you must have discipline. And motivation. Don't call us, we'll call you."

Vertag scowled to emphasize the difficulties ahead of candidates. "In the States," he went on, "the SSA is already a recognized charity organization with a multimillion-dollar turnover and impressive assets. That's in under two years. Now we're spreading through the rest of the West. In some ways God knows you guys need the SSA more than we do, particularly with regard to the political confrontation situation."

Malcolm's eyes were open now. Dougal thought it was probably because of the mention of dollars. The

8

multimillion-dollar turnover might also account for Hanbury's interest in the lecture, if any. Hanbury would enjoy benefiting from a registered charity.

Vertag had little more to say. He expressed a wish that his hearers should use their heads, strengthening the impression he had given of being doubtful of their capacity to do so. He glowered at the woman on his left and said that it gave him great pleasure to hand them back to the secretary of the British Apocalyptic Society.

The woman rose to her feet and thanked Dr. Vertag, reminding Dougal of a priestess attempting to pacify an unexpectedly hostile sacred cow. There would now be an interval for coffee, which would be followed, if Dr. Vertag would be so kind, by a time for the audience's questions.

She sat down and the audience allowed its pent-up coughs and sneezes to escape. A stout woman who had been sitting near Dougal at the back fetched a trolley-load of cups and saucers dominated by a gleaming coffee urn. The woman and her actions earthed the meeting in reality; Dougal felt that someone in a dog collar should propose a vote of thanks to her.

Vertag was served first. His nasal voice could be heard inquiring if they were certain this was coffee, because it sure as hell smelled like tea.

Dougal looked at Malcolm and gave a tiny jerk of his head in the direction of the door. Malcolm nodded and they both got to their feet.

"Hello . . ." The secretary of the British Apocalyptic Society was swooping down on them, as if she had scented the departure of potential prey. The hard sell clearly came unnaturally to her because there was an unhappy smile half concealed behind her thatch of hair. "You're new to the BAS, aren't you? So nice to see new faces."

"Yes." Dougal's fingers groped again toward his empty pocket. "It concerns us all, doesn't it? Fascinating lecture. But we must be off."

"I won't keep you," said the secretary desperately. She scrabbled in her brightly colored shoulder bag and produced a bundle of leaflets. "I'm sure you'd find these interesting."

Malcolm's hands were behind his back, but Dougal weakly accepted the stream of documents.

"That's the BAS charter, and that's the application form. Subscription rates are on the back. One of our leading members wrote this, he's on the steerage committee. It's about the political implications of the Apocalypse—it's awfully important, especially in a democratic society."

Dougal wondered if it would be less important in a totalitarian society and, if so, why? Words continued to spill out of the woman's mouth with a monotonous urgency that hinted at a long series of past rebuffs. Refusing the leaflets would be like kicking a stray dog looking for love.

"I'm afraid I have to ask you for a donation—we rely entirely on voluntary support. And I hope you're interested in joining us. Life membership really works out very cheaply."

Dougal could sense that Malcolm was on the verge of saying something rude, probably about the price of life membership. He swiftly produced a pound note.

"That'll do for both of us. Now we really must—"

"Hi, I'm Joe. Mary, I think Alex could do with another cup of coffee. I got some info here about the SSA, let me just give you a copy."

It was the freckled dignitary of the BAS who had been sitting on the right hand of Vertag. He wore oil-stained jeans and a yellow T-shirt that carried the mystifying legend GOD DRINKS AT CAMPERNOYLES ON HIS NIGHT OFF. WHY DON'T YOU? He thrust a glossy booklet into Dougal's hand. "We're distributing these as well, this evening. Dr. Vertag has only just got here from the States. What with jet lag and so on, he hasn't had time to sort out the Sealed Servants' back-up services."

"Thanks." Dougal took a step backward, closer to the door. He had taken an instant dislike to Joe, partly because he was so obviously the source of Mary's tentatively ruthless sales technique.

"We're late," Malcolm said, coming to Dougal's rescue. "Come on."

They nodded to Joe and left. As he turned, Dougal caught a curious expression on Joe's face: a look of surprise.

Why?

"So where's Hanbury?" Malcolm asked on the stairs to the street.

Dougal shrugged. "I don't feel like hanging around on the off chance of him turning up. How should I know where he is?" He realized that Hanbury's absence had made him angry; the perception itself increased his anger. "Let's go and find a drink."

The broad pavement outside was full of people. The air smelled of kebabs and exhaust fumes. There was a taxi parked by the curb. Dougal automatically looked to see if it was free. While he had money, he might as well use it.

As he did so, the cab's window slid open and the engine began to growl.

"William Dougal! *There* you are. And you must be Malcolm. Care for a lift?"

CHAPTER 2

"Taxis," said James Hanbury, "are the only way to get about in town."

Dougal looked at the back of Hanbury's neck. Had Hanbury hired, bought, or stolen the taxi? It looked exactly like an orthodox London black cab, with its own license number and a meter with thirty-eight pounds and few odd pence on it. He toyed with the idea that it was a kidnap vehicle with doors and windows controlled by a button on the dashboard. But the windows were down and the glass partition between front and back was open.

"You can park anywhere," Hanbury continued, "and drive up one-way streets and over zebra crossings that are littered with pedestrians. People simply don't notice you. Taxis are expected to behave like Soviet tanks in a hurry. The only problem is that you get besieged by would-be passengers whenever you stop. I got stuck in a jam by Harrods this afternoon and practically had to use force to repel a phalanx of Arab ladies."

Malcolm sighed loudly and lit a hand-rolled cigarette.

13

Dougal glanced out of the window and realized they had left the Harrow Road and come on to Marylebone High Street. He asked where they were going.

"I thought perhaps the Café Royal. Sadly changed, of course, but the cocktails are very reasonable. Have you eaten? We could have a snack in the grillroom."

The cigarette was a single-skin joint. Dougal's hyperactive sense of smell obligingly analyzed the smoke: Golden Virginia rolling tobacco and black hash—Pakistani, at a guess. If anything, prison had made Malcolm's habit of smoking dope in public more pronounced.

Malcolm nudged him, offering the joint. Dougal shook his head. He had no desire to get stoned, least of all in Hanbury's company. Besides, he belatedly realized, he had given up tobacco in all its forms.

The taxi nosed down Regent Street and parked within spitting distance of the canopy over the main entrance of the Café Royal. Malcolm got out and flicked the roach of his joint at a passing police car.

"Very witty," said Hanbury, in a tone of voice that meant *how childish*. It was the first sign he had shown of being aware of the joint. Dougal caught the spark of hostility in Hanbury's voice. It surprised him: Hanbury was far too sophisticated to show irritation—unless, of course, he intended to do so.

Hanbury led them through the revolving door into the hushed spaces of the hall. The doorman recognized him: he bowed to Hanbury without servility but with a certain respect. Hanbury nodded back. Dougal thought that in just such a way would a duke and an archbishop acknowledge one another's presence if they chanced to meet in the gents before having been formally introduced.

They went into the bar on the left. Hanbury led them to a corner table and chose for himself the seat best suited for observation of the room. Perhaps he did it out of habit.

Dougal pulled the dish of peanuts toward him and glanced around. He liked the Café Royal—not for the ornate splendors of the grillroom or the memories of Oscar Wilde, but for its unexpected spaciousness; you never felt cramped as you did in most of the places where people ate and drank in London.

Hanbury ordered a bottle of champagne. "After all, this is something of a celebration." He was wearing a lightweight beige-colored suit, a cream silk shirt, and a plain, dark brown tie. He was very tanned. He stared at his guests with a faint smile on his face.

"How did you know it was me?" The sharpness of the interruption and the slight thickening of Malcolm's tone suggested that the dope was taking effect.

Hanbury's mouth produced a boyish grin. "How much have you told him, William?"

"Enough." Dougal decided not to elaborate. Let Hanbury guess, it would be good for him.

"You know then that William invited me to look over your boat in your absence . . . funny little tub, isn't it? There was a photo of you lying around the cabin. And of course William had mentioned you and your, ah, little problems."

Why was Hanbury needling Malcolm? Dougal tried to squirt a little conversational oil on troubled waters by asking where Hanbury acquired his tan.

"Here and there. I was in the Caribbean for a while, but it becomes quite unbearable in July and August."

"Yes, dear." When Malcolm camped it up, it was a sure sign of irritation. "How sick making for you."

The waiter arrived with a bottle of Bollinger and three glasses. A second waiter followed with the ice bucket. Their silence was invaded by a burst of laughter from the next table, where a couple of tipsy businessmen were discussing their methods of retaining their bachelor freedoms while supporting wives and families.

Hanbury raised his glass. "To old friends, eh?" He took a quick sip. "You look very brown yourself, William. Where've you been?"

"We spent a few months in the Mediterranean with the *Sally-Anne*. For the last month we've been on Rhodes. Before I met Malcolm, I just bummed around Europe, Italy mainly." *And drank far too much red wine and brandy*. Dougal realized that Hanbury must already know most of this, certainly the latter part. The telegram to Rhodes and the telephone call last night implied that Hanbury had been keeping tabs on him. But Dougal was determined not to show any signs of curiosity or surprise. Hanbury fed like a vampire on the astonishment he so frequently engendered in his associates; it would do no harm to let him starve for a while.

Hanbury lit a cigarette and played with his glass. He commented—to Dougal—on the decor around them. Malcolm replied at length, leaning on the table and staring into Hanbury's eyes, using a favorite tactic for confusing unwanted listeners. His vowels and consonants began as cockney and shifted in midsentence to flattest Brum. He switched this to the sort of accent that suggests its user was not only born with a silver spoon in his mouth but has kept it there ever since. He ended with a West Country burr, addressing Hanbury as "Me Deario." Within these general categories, Malcolm added a further element of disturbance by varying his tone between the preternaturally grave and the unnaturally coy.

Dougal watched the mute hostility flickering between Malcolm and Hanbury. They were bickering like rival prima donnas. Perhaps their antipathies were based on their similarities. They both posed. They both adapted their circumstances to suit themselves.

And they both had killed, as easily as dogs kill rats.

Dougal drained his glass and set it down on the table with a clunk. The others fell silent and looked at him, as if waiting for their cues.

"Amanda," said Dougal. "How is she, James?"

"Fine as far as I know. I've not seen her for a while. Have you had no news of her at all?"

Dougal shook his head.

Hanbury pulled out his wallet and found a newspaper clipping nestling among the twenty-pound notes. "That's the last I've heard."

The typeface on the clipping belonged to *The Times*. It announced the bare fact that Bernard van der Gucht of Amsterdam and Miss Amanda Jackson of London intended to get married.

"Cigarette?" Hanbury offered his Caporals.

"No thanks." Dougal pushed the clipping back across the table, through a ring of champagne left by one of the glasses. The paper sucked at the liquid and broke into three soggy pieces.

"That was in late June," said Hanbury gently. "I hadn't seen her for weeks before that. But I knew which way the wind was blowing when Bernie gave her that pink Porsche of his."

Something in Hanbury's voice hinted that he hadn't taken the episode quite as lightheartedly as his words suggested. All things considered, he was behaving with uncharacteristic uncertainty this evening. He seemed unable to get down to business without prompting.

A tail-coated waiter gingerly ushered the two businessmen toward their dinner. All the adjacent tables were now empty.

"Now, James," Dougal said, "do tell us about the sale of the diamonds."

"Ah, yes. The diamonds." Hanbury sounded bemused, as if unsure which diamonds Dougal had in mind.

"How much did you get for them?"

"Nearly three hundred thousand dollars. In cash. It cost quite a lot to have it laundered, unfortunately."

"How do we split it? A third each?"

"There we have a problem." Hanbury contrived in a single, flowing movement to finish his champagne, to order another bottle from a passing waiter, and to look apologetic.

"Why?" Dougal distrusted Hanbury's problems as much as his figures.

"Amanda's got it. She said she needed a dowry. Bernie understood perfectly. As he was acting as the broker for the sale, I had little choice in the matter."

18

"I don't believe you." Dougal stated it as a fact, without animosity.

"Most of it," Hanbury conceded. "It's fair to say that Amanda and the, ah, incidental expenses have between them left us with very little profit."

"Load of old cobblers," remarked Malcolm judiciously. "Your nanny should wash your mouth out with soap for saying things like that."

Hanbury winced. "William, is it really necessary for us to have this—"

"Yes it is." Dougal smiled. "And you know the reason why. I don't trust you."

For an instant Hanbury's face crumpled like a child's on the verge of tears. Then he chuckled. "Fair enough, William."

The second bottle of Bollinger arrived and the conversation lapsed. Dougal realized that he was unlikely to get much further. Hanbury might be telling the truth. More probably, he was twisting it.

"James," said Dougal softly, "you know I can't believe something you say just because you say it. But I do want some of my share of the profits. I'd also like to know why you're pouring champagne down us. It can't be that you just want a captive audience for your hard luck story. Come to the point."

Dougal knew there must be a point somewhere— some coldly selfish reason for Hanbury's approach. He was enjoying the unexpected pleasures of being forthright. It not only induced a spurious moral self-satisfaction, but it also confused Hanbury.

Hanbury looked hurt. "Do credit me with some sense of responsibility, William. I couldn't leave you in the lurch. I've deposited ten thousand dollars in your name in an account in Geneva. Furthermore, I have five thousand pounds for you now. Believe me, I only wish it could have been more."

"It sounds too good to be true."

"I do have a quid pro quo in mind. Just a little one."

"You sure you don't mean a *sine qua non*?"

"Talk English," suggested Malcolm. "What's the catch?"

"There is a temporary snag," Hanbury admitted. "Even the largest financial institutions in the world occasionally have little problems with their cash flow. I too am subject to these, ah, hiccups in the global economy. However, I am on the verge of a coup, a little business venture that will remove the problem. For me and for you. Your assistance, William, would ensure a speedy and successful outcome. The whole affair is entirely legitimate of course. You would be in no danger and there would be no risk of legal repercussions."

"Didn't you say something like that last time?"

"That was completely different. Events got out of hand. And you became involved in the less satisfactory side of the affair entirely by your own choice." Hanbury extracted an envelope from his jacket pocket. "Look, have this in any case. It's a small token of my goodwill. At least allow me to outline my proposition."

Malcolm picked up the envelope from the table, lifted the flap, and peered inside. "You can't believe all you see. Probably Monopoly money. Or Bank of Toytown."

"Good God, man," hissed Hanbury, seemingly closer

to anger than Dougal had ever seen him, "what do you take me for? I'm not a *crook*."

"I'll check it. Note by note."

"I'm sure you've had plenty of experience."

"Where's the loo, William?" demanded Malcolm.

"Upstairs."

"I can't very well do it here. It won't take long." Malcolm stood up with some difficulty, leered belligerently at Hanbury, and left the room. Dougal smiled at his retreating back. Despite the dope and the fact that he had drunk most of the first bottle of champagne, Malcolm was still determined to guard Dougal's interests. And he was agreeably frank about his motive: it was a compound of altruism and greed.

"Thank God." The creases on Hanbury's forehead vanished. "I thought I'd never get rid of him. I always make it a rule never to blackmail people in front of witnesses."

CHAPTER 3

"If you're *sure* you can manage without me, I shall go to Paradise. Mind your cuddly friend doesn't take any liberties. Do you want this?" Malcolm waved the buff envelope, with its laboriously counted contents, in Dougal's direction.

Dougal shook his head. "You hang on to it. We'll sort it out later."

Since Malcolm had returned from the lavatory, the social temperature had dropped below freezing point, largely owing to his very reasonable unwillingness to believe that Dougal wanted to be alone with Hanbury. Dougal could tell that Malcolm was offended by his intention of going to Paradise. Being a romantic at heart, Malcolm usually avoided it. It was a gay disco north of the Bayswater Road that worked in much the same way as the Lonely Hearts column in *Private Eye*. He only went there when he was angry—or hurt—and generally found someone with a heart to spare for the night.

"Is he always like that—so abrasive?" Hanbury asked

when they were alone. "Or did prison warp a previously sunny character?"

"He just believes that attack is the best form of defense," replied Dougal dryly. "As a matter of fact, he rather enjoyed prison. He said he'd never had so many drugs in his life. Nor so many romantic opportunities. They made him librarian, and apparently the library is the nerve center of the black market. The only luxury he couldn't get was the sea. He got them to order the Kilmartin translation of Proust and managed to take it with him when he went."

Hanbury laughed. "A good-conduct prize, perhaps. He must be very adaptable." He paused to file the information away for future reference. "Tell me, is there— that is to say—are you—ah—what my American friends would call a *bi-guy*?" He enunciated the word as if it tasted of cod liver oil.

"Don't worry, James. Malcolm offers to seduce me about once a year, but I've always refused."

There was a silence. Hanbury looked embarrassed, as if he had been betrayed into showing a superfluous emotion. Dougal used the opportunity to replay what Hanbury had said while Malcolm was counting the money upstairs.

"There's a reason why cooperation would be in your interest. You see, Amanda told me what happened to that little tramp in Rosington. I made a point of checking back through the local newspaper files. It was an open verdict. Neither the police nor the coroner was very happy. They would welcome further information. Don't you think we should continue this conversation without the benefit of a third party?"

Pillow talk, Dougal thought bitterly. Only Amanda

had known what had happened. Oh, it had been self-defense all right—but who was going to believe that? If they could pin it on him, he would be lucky to escape with a verdict of manslaughter.

"Don't look so worried," Hanbury said. "Would you like some food? I always find that settling the stomach helps to settle the mind. No? I don't want you to do anything criminal. Just something that's important to me. And you won't regret it financially. There was a thousand pounds in that envelope. You'll get a further four thousand on completion of contract. A week or two after that, I'll give you the passbook to your very own Swiss bank account."

Dougal stared at his glass. The bubbles in the wine were straining upward to the air. He felt as if he had allowed Hanbury to build a cage around him. There was no point in snarling at the outside world through the bars. It was his own fault; he should have ignored the telegram and the phone call and trusted his instincts. He pushed his glass away from him: the champagne tasted sour. He was tempted to scrounge one of Hanbury's Caporals but denied himself the pleasure on the grounds that it was necessary to retain a scrap of self-respect.

"All I want you to do, William, is to undertake a little surveillance. Just for a few days—a week or two at the outside. I've arranged all the preliminary details. The only thing you need to do is—ah—survey."

"If you want someone watched, and it's entirely legitimate, why don't you use a private detective? It's what they're trained for. And they don't cost as much as you say you're going to pay me."

Hanbury beamed. "Good question. I can't tell you how much pleasure it gives me to work with you again. Most people would have ignored that angle. Greed blinds them, you see. Do you know any private detectives?"

Dougal shook his head.

"I think I may say that my acquaintance with them has been extensive over the years. Ninety percent of them are retired policemen. They tend to be stolid, flat-footed, and better in the witness-box than in the field. I need someone who can blend into the background—the sort of background you will have observed tonight at that lecture. Tell me, how did the audience strike you?"

Dougal thought for a moment. "Predominantly white middle class, I suppose, plus a sprinkling of the lunatic fringe. Most of them were probably in their twenties. Educated but not yet well off."

"Exactly. And you would have no difficulty in pretending to be one of them. Perhaps the subject really *does* interest you. We're all waiting for the end of the world in one way or another. In any case, I'm sure you have the necessary intellectual equipment to make small talk about Armageddon, nuclear proliferation, and so forth. You'll find it child's play. No orthodox private detective would be able to do that part of the job so well. As for the financial aspect, I know I'm paying you over the odds. But in your case I *want* to be generous—you know what the Bard says:

> . . . *it is twice bless'd:*
> *It blesseth him that gives and him that takes.'* "

Hanbury paused, as if to admire the aptness of the quotation.

"I think Shakespeare was referring to the quality of mercy. Not that it matters." It was difficult to credit Hanbury with the possession of a conscience, let alone a guilty one; all the evidence lay in the other direction. "What do you want me to do—join the British Apocalyptic Society?"

"It wouldn't do any harm. But your real interest must be the Sealed Servants of the Apocalypse. More precisely, I want you to keep an eye on its president, Alexander Vertag. Just while he's in this country. His main purpose for being here is to study the feasibility of establishing a branch of the SSA in England. He arrived early, which is why the BAS invited him to be their guest speaker at such short notice. Quite a bonus from our point of view, though it did prevent me from introducing you to Joe Graver."

"Graver? The BAS man with freckles?" Like a ferret in glasses, Dougal thought. He remembered that odd expression of surprise on Joe's face when they left.

"He introduced himself to you?"

"Yes, he came up just as we were going. Gave us some stuff on the SSA."

"He's a good boy," said Hanbury unexpectedly. "I wanted you two to meet because he'll be sponsoring your application to join the SSA. I would have been there myself if he hadn't rung to say that Vertag had turned up early. That's why I had to wait outside. You see, Vertag wants a British amanuensis while he's on his—ah—fact-finding mission in this country. That's going to be you."

26

"How can you be so sure?"

Hanbury shrugged modestly. "Certainty is an impossible ideal. But one can generally contrive to arrange the probabilities into a very good imitation of it. You can leave that to me. But it was just as well that Vertag didn't see us chatting away like old friends in his audience."

Dougal frowned and kept silent. He could see that Hanbury wanted him to supply a comment, a cue. Refusing to do so might bring him to the point.

The tactic worked. Hanbury abandoned his preferred method of exposition—the Socratic dialogue, with himself in the role of Socrates—and tersely announced that he was representing American business interests that were in the process of negotiating with a consortium that Vertag controlled in the United States. Hanbury's employers suspected that Vertag might attempt to back out and arrange an alternative transaction in the United Kingdom. Dougal's task was to monitor Vertag's movements and report them to Hanbury.

"Why can't you do it yourself?"

Hanbury sighed. "Vertag's a silly little man. We met before in another context. He's got it into his head that I'm working for the CIA."

CHAPTER 4

Friday morning began with a cough like a gasping vacuum cleaner. The vacuum cleaner was trapped inside Dougal's chest and was trying to get out by way of his head.

Dougal opened his eyes to see if that would help. Bright, harsh sunlight was pouring through the skylight. He closed his eyes and pulled the sheet over his head.

Sun through the skylight meant it was already mid to late morning. Days had never begun like this when he was smoking. There was usually a morning tickle, but nothing the first cigarette of the day couldn't handle.

When the cough stopped, Dougal was able to confirm what he already suspected: it was a fallacy that champagne never gave you a hangover. He slid his arm from under the sheet and cautiously swept the bedside table. He found the Paracetamol and eventually succeeded in prying off the lid. He sent his arm back for the water. His funny bone came into contact with the edge of the table. The glass slid out of his fingers and shattered.

Dougal lay still and considered what he should do. On the whole he would prefer to go back to sleep, but the headache and the sunshine made this difficult. Then the memory of last night's events began to trickle through his mind. They were jumbled like fragments of a dream. They routed the possibility of sleep entirely and made the headache worse.

A key turned in the lock of the front door. Steps crossed the sitting room. The bedroom door was jerked open.

"God," said Malcolm. "You're wasting time again. Coffee and muesli in five minutes, okay?"

Dougal felt the injustice of the remark. Malcolm had the constitution of a rhinoceros and in any case rarely wanted more than four or five hours' sleep. Malcolm's luxuriant store of vitality acted as a constant reproach to Dougal's more modest supply. Nevertheless he forced himself to get up and, five minutes later, joined Malcolm in the sitting room. The sight of Malcolm savaging a mound of muesli in a soup bowl drove him into the tiny kitchen to make the coffee. As an afterthought he poured himself some orange juice. With a glass in one hand and a mug in the other, he would have nowhere to put the cigarette his body was demanding.

Malcolm said nothing when Dougal rejoined him. Dougal realized that the dismissal yesterday evening had not been forgotten. Nor forgiven.

"Had a good night?"

"Had worse." Malcolm scraped his bowl with the

mournful concentration of someone wondering if he should throw delicacy to the winds and replace the spoon with his tongue. "It went on too long. This guy laid a gigantic line of coke on me at five o'clock. It wasn't worth trying to go to sleep." He sniffed, partly for nostalgia, partly from necessity, and wholly with pride: smug sniffing was one of the distinguishing marks of a cocaine user.

Malcolm put down his bowl and sipped his coffee. Dougal realized that he would have to tell him what had happened. It would be better to do it now, while his hangover was dwarfing the importance of everything else.

He stared at the blue blank of sky framed by the window and explained that his unfriendly behavior last night was forced upon him by Hanbury's blackmail. He described the death of the tramp in that decaying house in Rosington. "He rolled on his own knife, you know. But who would believe that?" Sometimes, when nightmares molded memories in the defenselessness of sleep, Dougal had difficulty believing it himself. "And afterward I tried to mock up a suicide." He shivered. "I couldn't think of anything else to do."

"What went wrong?" The reserve had vanished from Malcolm's manner. He was leaning forward, his coffee forgotten.

Dougal outlined Amanda's inconvenient indiscretion and Hanbury's investigations. The price of Hanbury's silence seemed moderate. Malcolm commented that no doubt Hitler's demand for *lebensraum* had seemed very reasonable at first glance.

"And I start tonight," Dougal finished. "Joe's got a

30

wine bar in Camden called Campernoyles. Remember the T-shirt? I've got to go there tonight and meet Vertag. And telephone a report to Hanbury every twelve hours—sooner, if anything important happens."

Malcolm's immediate reaction was to advise flight. They now had money and they could be out of the country in a few hours. Hanbury must be bluffing: if he put the finger on Dougal, there was nothing to stop Dougal putting it on Hanbury in return. Hanbury would have little to gain and much to lose by being vindictive. "You're just small-fry, William. He'd never bother with *revenge*." He made the word sound faintly ridiculous and rather vulgar, like the routine rhetoric of a Jacobean monster.

Dougal shook his head. "I thought of that last night. But it wouldn't work. I'd spend all my time waiting for Hanbury to do something. It'd be life under a suspended sentence of death. Besides, he's not just a cozy little crook like the ones you're used to. It's safer to assume that Hanbury's a cross between Moriarty and Superman until proved otherwise."

Despite Malcolm's opposition, Dougal refused to change his mind. He was sure that Hanbury would have allowed for the possibility of a doublecross.

"Just what do you propose to do?" Malcolm was beginning to get angry. His shirts were always too small for him; when he was enraged it was as if his body was trying to burst out of his clothes. "As far as I can see you'll have to kill the bloody man if you want to be safe."

"No." Dougal's head felt hot and feverish. A malign Fate had put it on the stove and was stirring hard with a wooden spoon. Malcolm's reasoning was frighteningly familiar.

"Oh come on, don't be stupid. We both know it's sometimes the best solution. We needn't get involved. There's a little family firm in Dagenham that specializes in contracts. Expensive, but—"

"No more killing," said Dougal firmly. He had lost most of his moral qualms about murder recently. But not all of them. Besides, it wasn't the best solution as far as he was concerned. It would cause other problems and generate more nightmares. He knew he would be unable to make Malcolm understand this. One of the unspoken preconditions of their oddly enduring friendship was that it was founded on a shared inability to understand each other.

It was easy to supply a more acceptable explanation: Hanbury was an experienced exponent of the art of lethal one-upmanship; trying to kill him could so easily backfire.

"If I do what he wants," Dougal continued, "I might be able to outmaneuver him . . ." His voice stopped of its own accord. Dougal recognized he was trying to persuade himself as much as Malcolm. And failing on both counts.

"If pigs had wings," said Malcolm rudely. "I'm getting out of harm's way."

Part of Dougal's mind cleared: a temporary patch of lucidity in the middle of fear and hangover. "There's one thing you can do. We're only taking Hanbury's word that the police are still interested in the tramp's death. Could you go up to Rosington and try to find out? All you'd have to do is check the local papers and keep your ears open. Find a friendly policeman. Talk to strange men in pubs."

Malcolm smiled, baring his strong yellow teeth in a leer. "I'll enjoy that."

Dougal's flat was in the attic. Two floors of bedsitters insulated him from his landlady's flat on the ground floor. Dougal was grateful that architectural circumstances kept them apart. He owed Mrs. Moran six weeks' rent. He found it pleasant to reflect that the thousand pounds Hanbury had given him would enable him to pay this debt. He disliked owing money to old-age pensioners, and his guilt was reinforced every time he skulked in and out of the house trying to avoid being intercepted by her.

Dougal saw Malcolm off just before 1:00 P.M. He squared his shoulders, crossed the cool, chequer-flagged hall, and tapped on the door of Mrs. Moran's sitting room.

Mrs. Moran was sitting in a wing armchair. Her Persian cat, Mrs. Twiddle, was purring on her lap. Mrs. Twiddle was arguably the most selfish animal that Dougal had ever met; the Mrs. was a courtesy title, for Mrs. Moran preferred to save lower species from the consequences of their own sexuality.

"Hallo, Mrs. Moran. I—"

"William! How nice to see you. Dear me, you *are* brown. I thought you were back, but I wasn't sure. You didn't drink the water, I hope? Pour us both a glass of sherry and come and tell me all about it. Was your hotel comfortable?"

Dougal crossed to the sideboard, an ornate piece of

33

furniture that would not have looked out of place in a banqueting hall. He was puzzled by Mrs. Moran's affability. It was true that she liked him, largely because she erroneously supposed that Dougal was as Scottish as herself. But he would have expected his arrears of rent to have brought out another of her Scottish characteristics: despite the fact that Mrs. Moran was eighty-two and could be moved to tears by the sight of a kitten with a pink ribbon round its neck, she knew to a penny how much her tenants owed her and usually became increasingly irritated by any delay in receiving her just deserts.

Dougal poured two glasses of the straw-colored sherry in the decanter. He knew from experience that it would be good—very dry and very smooth. Mrs. Moran's domestic economies did not affect her sherry.

He gave her a glass of sherry and smiled down at her. It never failed to surprise him that Mrs. Moran so closely resembled the Platonic ideal of the perfect grandmother, from her fluffy white hair with its discreet blue rinse to her slim black patent leather shoes.

Mrs. Moran's voice—as dry and smooth as the sherry—rustled over the events of the last few months. Mrs. Twiddle had eaten an entire quarter pound of salmon that Mrs. Moran had inadvertently left out on the kitchen table. That nice Matilda Brown ("first floor back, dear") had kindly cleared Mrs. Moran's back garden. She had had to be very firm about the rabbit next door, very firm indeed. It was for its own good. She wished people would put their rubbish in plastic bags before putting it in the dustbin.

Dougal allowed his attention to wander. Mrs. Twiddle's purring blended with Mrs. Moran's gentle conversation. *A lullaby for two larynges.* His eyelids were drooping. He shifted in his chair, trying to reach the roll of notes in his pocket.

". . . and such a nice man, too. Of course with a name like Stuart, you'd expect it. That family always had charm if nothing else, don't you agree?"

Dougal nodded obediently, wondering whom she meant. A new lodger or an old friend? It was often hard to tell with Mrs. Moran: her mind made little distinction between past and present.

He finished his sherry and managed to interrupt Mrs. Moran for long enough to tell her that he must settle the rent he owed, while he was here.

Mrs. Moran's reply bewildered him: "No, dear, hasn't he told you? You're up-to-date now." She allowed a wistful note to creep into her voice. "Of course, if you want to pay for a few weeks in advance, it might be simpler for you."

Dougal reached into his pocket. "Who hasn't told me? I don't follow."

"Mr. Stuart. Your uncle. Such a thoughtful man. Not many men would bother to see if all was well at a nephew's flat. But I'm surprised he hasn't been in touch with you. He asked me to telephone him when you got back. He had some good news for you."

"Oh, I have seen him," Dougal said quickly. "Last night in fact. He must have forgotten to mention the rent." Dougal's parents were only children; there was just one candidate for the role of honorary uncle. It solved one minor mystery: how Hanbury had known that Dougal was home. "Which reminds me, could I check his phone number? I've lost it."

Mrs. Moran directed Dougal to the pad beside the telephone. The number she had written was the same as the one Hanbury had given him last night. Above it was the name James F. E. Stuart.

The Old Pretender. Who but James Hanbury would choose a pseudonym that so clearly announced itself as such?

The thought of Hanbury roaming around his flat without a chaperon was less amusing. Inspecting a person's possessions in his absence gave you an unfair advantage over him—an unlicensed intimacy. Panic dispelled the last of Dougal's hangover. Hanbury might have planted a voice-activated microphone in the flat. In which case, he would know that he couldn't trust Dougal and that Malcolm had gone to Rosington.

Dougal tried to dismiss his fears as the melodramatic products of reading too much pulp fiction. But they refused to leave, for the simple reason that Hanbury *was* melodramatic; he produced, directed, acted and watched his own performances.

CHAPTER 5

"If this is the house white," Dougal said, "you'd better give me a glass of that Macon Blanc instead." The house white had the color of fresh engine oil; it probably shared other characteristics too. Besides, there was a sporting chance that Hanbury might cover his expenses.

The fat man behind the bar quivered. The lower buttons of his shirt were undone, and Dougal could see rolls of hairy fat vibrating within.

"Yes, sir." The man's voice was as dull as a rusted nail.

Dougal stared with clinical interest at the barman's drooping posterior. It was curious to see a fat person looking so woebegone: you expected bulky people to be cheerful. This one looked like a very worried thin person clothed in someone else's ill-fitting, cast-off fat. As the barman turned, with the overflow from Dougal's glass of Macon dripping down his fingers, Dougal noticed the startling blue of his eyes. He looked closer and saw that the pupils had contracted to the brink of invisibility.

That was odd. Campernoyles was not well lit: the management had supplemented the fading daylight with nothing more than a few candles.

"You'll need the menu." The fat man pushed a handwritten white card, enveloped in plastic, across the imitation marble bar top.

"I'm not hungry." Dougal felt his irritation returning.

"I'm afraid sir will have to have *something*, if only for the look of it. It's the terms of our license, you see."

"All right," said Dougal, trying not to blame the barman for circumstances manifestly beyond his control, "I'll have a slice of that quiche. Please."

"Crusty wholewheat pastry and organic mushrooms," the fat man intoned, his attention wandering away from Dougal while habit kept him quoting from the menu. "Fresh free-range eggs from our farm in Gloucestershire. Herbs handpicked from a genuine Tudor—"

"Just a small slice," said Dougal firmly.

The sales talk stopped. Dougal had the strange feeling that it was entirely unrelated to the barman; the words were using his mouth in much the same way as a garrulous dead soul hijacks the lips of a medium.

Dead soul: zombie. It was not a comforting analogy.

While the fat man stabbed at a quiche at the far end of the counter, Dougal looked around. Campernoyles of Camden Town inhabited a converted shop.

The frontage was dominated by a plate-glass window on which bunches of bright red grapes had been painted, interspersed with extremely yellow ears of corn. Just inside the window, the obligatory row of wilting cheese plants enhanced the gloom. The counter was flanked by a line of wicker-covered bar stools whose backs bit viciously into your spine. The floor—bare boards with a sprinkling of ethnic sawdust and the leftovers of yesterday's snacks—was crammed with fragile tables and chairs of stripped pine. The peeling walls were decorated with mirrors advertising defunct ales and stouts.

God was not in evidence tonight; perhaps it wasn't His night off. A dozen people were sipping, nibbling, and talking at the tables. The clientele resembled the audience at last night's lecture—young, white, and impoverished.

The barman returned with a gray triangle of quiche nestled on a large, brown-rimmed lettuce leaf. Dougal paid him and raised a hand to detain him.

"By the way," he said, "I'm looking for Joe Graver." He laid the completed application forms on the counter. "The British Apocalyptic Society. The Sealed Servants."

The fat man dropped the five-pound note he was holding. It fluttered behind the counter. His features twitched anarchically, as if the muscles behind them had lost their coordination.

"*Don't join*," he whimpered.

"Why not?" Dougal began. "I thought—"

"That's okay, Bert. I'll take over."

Joe Graver's approach had been masked by the barman's bulk; he materialized with shocking suddenness at Bert's elbow.

"Hi, it's Bill Dougal, isn't it? We met last night. Bert, you could do with a break. You've been out here since we opened. Get Mary to take over."

Bert backed away. Joe bent down, retrieved Dougal's fiver, and tossed it on the bar. "On the house."

Dougal tried to smile his thanks. "I gather I should be meeting Dr. Vertag here. James said—"

Joe shook his head with a violence that set his wiry curls bouncing. "For God's sake, leave James out of it, man. Alex needs an aide while he's in this country, and I'll just introduce you as an old friend." He whisked Dougal's BAS application form out of sight. "You've been one of our members for years, okay? But no one except me knows you because you don't live in London. You do the job, and I keep my nose clean. I don't want to know what James is up to—he gave me his word that it wouldn't affect the BAS or harm Alex, and that's all I care about."

"Fair enough. Is Vertag here?"

"Not yet. Any moment now." Joe abruptly switched his tack. "I hope Bert didn't freak you. He's a bit weird, but I feel kind of responsible for him—he's been with us since we opened this place. He's not usually out front, but we're short tonight. I guess we all got our problems."

Mary—the BAS woman with the pendulous breasts—came out to deal with the customers. Joe helped himself to a glass of orange juice with the enigmatic remark that there was nothing he liked better than a glass of O J; A J and P J just weren't the same. He talked to Dougal about the aims and the achievements of the BAS. A particular source of pride was the fallout shelter they planned to build in Powys. It became clear as he talked that he regarded the Sealed Servants with respect, some of which rubbed off on Vertag. "You got to hand it to Alex, he thinks big. He's made the SSA into just about the most important Apocalyptic organization on either side of the Atlantic. Their detailed planning's amazing, and he's brilliant at fund raising. . . ." There was even talk of the eventual amalgamation of the two organizations, which Joe hinted was partly the reason for Vertag's presence in this country. "Trouble is, they're so big—we'd lose our identity. I'd be an executive V.P. with control over the Western European sector, but it wouldn't be the same. . . ."

Dougal goaded Joe with the occasional leading question and watched him talk. Like Bert, Joe was nervous. But Bert's state probably derived from an inadequate supply of opiates, whereas Joe's was harder to diagnose. His eyes were never still: they darted all over the room—in search of Vertag? His accent was flat and classless, overlaid with the nostalgic mid-Atlantic idioms of an aging hippie. Joe was worried, and probably hiding something, Dougal concluded. Too devious for his own good? On the other hand, Dougal didn't doubt Joe's sincerity in one respect: he believed that Armageddon was overdue and that he and his associate Vertag could, if not avert it, at least salvage something from the catastrophe.

Dougal was torn between uncomfortably contradictory impulses: he wanted to laugh at his host's presumption; yet it was arguably a more praiseworthy aim in life than his own uncomplicated hedonism. If Vertag proved to be as dedicated as Joe, there should be little difficulty in pretending a similar devotion for a week or two. Everyone remade the world in his own image: Vertag would be predisposed to accept Dougal's sympathy with the aims of the SSA because it would mirror his own.

"Had we better settle the details of our previous acquaintance?" Dougal asked. "It would be silly to risk awkward questions—"

The door of the wine bar was pushed open with enough violence to knock over one of the cheese plants and reduce half a dozen conversations to silence. Vertag strode swiftly to the bar and slammed down a book beside Joe's glass. Ignoring Dougal, he leaned over the counter.

"Damn it, man, I just don't need this." His green eyes glowed angrily at Joe. "I haven't got the time to waste on a bunch of mystics. You said it was worth contacting your Hackney group. 'Dynamic potential,' you said. Dynamic crap. The first thing they did was give me this." His finger stabbed the shoddily produced paperback between them. "Those guys believe every word. You know what it's about? *Arthur*. King Arthur rides again. They really think that all they have to do is sit on their asses and wait for the round table to reappear. Then all our trouble will be over. Jesus!"

Joe cleared his throat. "Look, Alex, I'm sorry. A lot of our people tend to go a bit over the top on the mystic angle. I guess it sort of motivates them to—"

"No way, Joe. No way am I having nostalgia freaks like that. We may have to rethink our entire UK strategy if those guys are typical of the BAS. They're looking back to the mumbo jumbo of the past because they're scared of the future. Give me some bourbon."

Joe, with an expression on his face that reminded Dougal of a beaten dog, produced a bottle of Jim Beam, a half-pint tumbler, and an ice bucket. "Alex, this is Bill Dougal, the guy I mentioned. Knows this country like the back of his hand. Lots of organizing experience. Degree in business management. He's just what you need while you're here."

Vertag took a long swallow of his whiskey. "Hi," he said unenthusiastically. "I hope he's an improvement on your buddies in Hackney." He turned to Dougal. "I suppose I'd better talk to you. Come on over here."

He led the way to a table at the back of the room, leaving Dougal to follow with the ice bucket, the bottle, and his own glass. Joe spread the palms of his hands toward Dougal, as if to say, "Over to you. I've done all I can."

Dougal lowered himself cautiously onto the rickety chair. Vertag was staring into space, muttering with subdued violence about mysticism. Even when seated, Vertag's restless energy was apparent. Dougal thought he was the sort of person who spent his waking hours vibrating like an emotional tuning fork. God knew what his dreams were like. Hanbury should have warned him that Vertag would need careful handling. It suddenly occurred to Dougal that if Vertag refused to take him on Hanbury would have to let him off

43

the hook. It would hardly be Dougal's fault. It would need to be done carefully, of course, for their conversation might get back to Hanbury through Joe.

Dougal drained his wine, put an ice cube in his glass, and reached for the bottle of Jim Beam. Vertag looked up, his lips parted in surprise. Dougal felt a bubble of laughter rising inside him: Vertag clearly was not accustomed to potential subordinates who took liberties.

"You're making a mistake," Dougal said, once he had captured his audience. "In the short term, mystics make excellent cannon fodder, precisely because their thinking is so woolly. You can't have an organization entirely made up of generals. Hitler used the cranks in the twenties and then discarded them when he had no need for them. Think what the technique did for him." *Set him on the road to a suicide in a concrete bunker.*

But Vertag was smiling. "You got a point, Bill." His eyes narrowed. "It's good to hear a bit of fresh thinking for once. As a matter of fact, I've been considering a two-tier approach too. An elite group of survivors, supported by a disposable work force. Trouble is, the policy would be hard to implement in terms of existing structures like the BAS. Too many amateur cowboys at every level."

"I would have thought that survival's just a minor preliminary," said Dougal, arrogantly if illogically. "Your real problem will come afterward. I haven't seen much evidence of, ah, forward planning on that score."

"Right." Vertag sounded as enthusiastic as ever. "That's a flaw shared by most of our sister organizations—including the BAS. But not the SSA. Our long-

44

term projections recognize that we're on the threshold of a new era. It'll affect everything, man, from geopolitical externals to the inner depths of the human mind. I'm really interested in the implications for psychotherapy. Western society as a whole is psychosexually at the anal stage. We'll have to clear away the traumas of millennia."

"And how do you propose to reach a position where you can take control? Nothing you've said so far suggests that you've got the means to convert fantasy into reality."

Vertag stared at him. For a moment Dougal thought that his abrasiveness had had the desired effect. "Joe was right," he said slowly. "You've got a mind like a laser. And aggressive, huh? I like it. Let me explain. In broad terms, our structure is based on the revolutionary cell grouping. It's already working well back in the States. One of our contact people initiates interest in a given area through a program of lectures, courses, and media events. Then he or she selects local people who are capable of running their group. We run a pretty thorough check on them first, of course. The contact issues broad guidelines and sets up a two-way communication procedure. The cell leader always reports back to the contact, who in turn reports to the Central Executive."

"Isn't that rather unnecessarily secretive?"

"It's *crucial*, Bill. Partly because we want to preserve the personal element in the chain of command. No faceless bureaucrats for us. But the main reason is that we have to keep in mind the possibility of state intervention. What we're doing is too realistic for the liking of our rulers. They just want a quiet, uncomplaining electorate that does what it's told and ignores the future. We've had the Feds sniffing around the SSA, you know. And the IRS tinkering with our tax returns. The BAS has no security worth the name, but I reckon your Special Branch already knows that."

Vertag sat back, his laughter lines biting deep into his suntan. Dougal, who had assessed him as a fanatic with fascist leanings, suddenly revised his opinion. Vertag had charm. Like Hanbury, he could turn it on and off at will. At this moment, he was sending waves of attraction toward Dougal. This scared Dougal more than anything so far. Vertag was more than an articulate crank; he was dangerous.

"Now let me ask some questions." Vertag pushed the bottle of Jim Beam across the table. "Joe's filled me in on your general background." Dougal wished that Joe had done the same for him. *Damn Hanbury.* "Two degrees," Vertag obligingly continued, "now unemployed but with a background in local government administration with the London Borough of—"

"Pseudocivil service," Dougal interrupted hastily, before the conversation could become awkwardly specific. He parenthetically enjoyed Vertag's pronunciation of the word *borough*, which suggested, not inappropriately, the residence of rabbits. "Amazingly petty. I had to get out."

"Okay, okay." Vertag dismissed the subject of Dougal's fictional past with a wave of his hand. "What I really want to know is what's motivating you. Why do you want to join the SSA?"

Dougal stared at Vertag. It was his last chance to

46

alienate Vertag without Hanbury being able to say that he had done it intentionally. "Civilization's got maybe twenty years to go, in its present form," he began. "You haven't convinced me of that—I knew it already." He paused, as if dredging the depths of his mind for its most profound conclusions. *Gently.* Vertag was an idealist of sorts, so a little selfish pragmatism was called for. "To be honest, I just want to survive. I don't give a toss for anyone else. The only reason I'm interested in the SSA is that it offers the most realistic chance of survival. No more, no less." *Take it or—preferably—leave it.*

Vertag's quick nod destroyed Dougal's hopes.

"Right, Bill, *right*. I'm in it for the same reason. I always ask people that question. The answer always sorts out the fools and the frauds. You wouldn't believe how many people are waiting for the age of Aquarius. Self-interest is the only viable motive. Shit, man, that's what evolution's all about. Right?"

"Right." Dougal dedicated the next few seconds to loathing himself in silence. He'd mishandled the interview from the start. If he had had a cigarette, he would have lit it. What did it matter? He reached for the bourbon.

Vertag started to explain his plans. He intended to spend a week or ten days touring Britain, meeting local BAS representatives, and assessing the potential impact of the SSA. "Basically, it'll be a whistle-stop fact-finding mission, Bill. I need you to sort out the itinerary, make travel arrangements, and fill me in on the background. I also have to see a few business contacts while I'm here. I'll pay you a fee for two weeks' work—it'll be round-the-clock, remember. At the end of that time we'll know more about each other and we can discuss the future." Vertag sent another burst of charm across the table. "If we work well together, this could mean something big for you. We're thinking of establishing a London-based SSA secretariat, plus a channel for US-UK liaison. Think about it, huh?"

Dougal was thinking about it. He also thought about Hanbury and the disturbing advice of Bert the barman: *"Don't join."*

CHAPTER 6

The yellow glare of street lamps turned Camden Town into a network of brick-and-glass canyons huddled beneath an improbably purple sky. It was well after midnight, and there was little traffic on the road. Dougal crossed to the pavement diagonally opposite Campernoyles and looked back at the wine bar he had just left.

The braless girl with caterpillar brows was lethargically stacking chairs on tables. At each table she swiftly drained the bottles and glasses remaining on them. Otherwise the room was empty. Dougal felt surprisingly alert, considering his intake of bourbon. It was a relief to be alone again after a long evening exclusively devoted to making the appropriate conversational responses to Alex Vertag and Joe Graver. He realized that there was yet another hidden catch to his little job for Hanbury.

It was going to be excruciatingly boring.

At least he had a few hours to himself. Vertag had asked him to return to Campernoyles at five o'clock

tomorrow afternoon, suitably equipped for a trip round
the major cities of Great Britain. Joe would perhaps
join them in the second week.

Don't join.

Too many reservations nagged at Dougal. It wasn't
just Bert's warning—though that was disturbing
enough in this context—but the enthusiasm with
which both Vertag and Graver had accepted him. Dougal wasn't unduly modest, and he realized that many
Americans approached a new acquaintance with an
undisguised rapture that seemed alien to Europeans;
the latter were accustomed to relationships that evolved
in a more leisurely fashion.

It had all been so easy.

Vertag himself was puzzling—that unexpected
charm allied to his frequently mentioned conviction
that most of the human race was disposable. Joe, too,
seemed to accept this proposition without blinking;
his attitude toward Vertag was clearly one of covert
hero worship.

Leaning in the doorway of a steel-shuttered hi-fi
shop, Dougal tried to analyze his distrust of them. He
was inclined to attribute it to the fact that they were
so clearly organization men; they acted and thought
as group leaders, not as individuals.

Pack animals, like wolves. Dougal shivered, despite the
warmth of the night air, and then wanted to laugh
at his own pomposity. It was time to go home. It was
a fair walk from Camden Town to West Hampstead,
but he realized that he would be unlikely to pick up
a taxi at this time of night.

He was about to move off in the direction of Chalk

Farm when the roar of engines in a confined space distracted him. The sound funneled out from the dark mouth of an alley immediately to the right of Campernoyles.

Dougal pulled himself farther back into the shadow of the doorway. The noise increased. Suddenly a pair of headlights appeared, throwing the alley into sharp relief. Dougal received a brief impression of cobblestones pushing up through patchy gray asphalt. Weeds that lined the narrow passage threw menacing shadows up the walls. A serpentine bracket projected from the lefthand wall, the rusting support of a long-vanished gas lamp.

The harsh white light of the headlamps concealed the vehicle behind them until it turned on to the main road. The bulky shape resolved itself into an eighteen-hundredweight van. It moved rapidly down the deserted street in the direction of Euston. Dougal could just make out the words on the side of the van: CAMPERNOYLES FRUIT & VEGETABLES.

Another van—a twin of the first—followed a few seconds later. Dougal caught sight of the year letter on the registration plate. It was this year's model. Campernoyles must be doing better than the interior of the wine bar suggested.

The questions immediately began to form in Dougal's mind, corroding like acid. How much spare capital did two brand new eighteen-hundredweight vans represent? Why had no one mentioned that Campernoyles was more than just a wine bar? Where were they going to at this hour of the morning? It was far too early for Covent Garden.

Something and nothing. Dougal knew he could supply half a dozen explanations. But, adding the vans to the other events of the evening, they did nothing to assuage his growing uneasiness.

The last light in the wine bar disappeared. All three stories of the Campernoyles frontage were in darkness. Dougal found he was recrossing the road before he had made a conscious decision to do so.

He slipped into the mouth of the alley and stood in the darkness, forcing himself to wait until his eyes had grown accustomed to the lack of light. His pulse had accelerated. He made a bid for self-control with slow, deep breathing, but the air still rustled through his nostrils in ragged little gasps.

There were still cars and a few passersby on the main road, but they seemed to belong to another country. Nowhere is quite as lonely as the night in London.

Details crept out of the darkness. The tops of the windowless buildings on either side, outlined against the purple sky, had always been visible. But now Dougal could pick out the parallel lines of the curb stones and a network of drainpipes on the building to the right.

He was afraid, of course—partly of the unknown that lay waiting for him up the alleyway, and partly of seeming ridiculous; he couldn't rid himself of the idea that he might be scared for no purpose. One reason alone kept him here: ironically enough, his instinct for self-preservation. It occurred to him that Hanbury might think he was being conscientious.

He began to move up the alleyway. Each step was followed by a pause for listening. Once he stumbled and could barely restrain himself from running back to the road. He counted each step and translated them to yards. It preserved the illusion of progress.

The light flashed on when he was between nineteen and twenty. Dougal threw himself against the wall and bit his lip, as if the pain could exorcise the risk of discovery.

Little by little, his panic subsided. The light must belong to a room at the back of Campernoyles. It enabled Dougal to see most of the far end of the alley. It was a cul-de-sac lined with brick walls, with the exception of the twenty-yard gap between Campernoyles and the end. This was blocked with a fence of wire mesh, in the center of which was the gate the vans had used.

Dougal moved forward to the junction of Campernoyles and the fence. The yard beyond was surprisingly large. Its rear boundary was formed by three pairs of heavy wooden doors, presumably leading to garages.

He inched up to the gate, which was secured by two padlocks. Barbed wire glinted along the top of the fence. The overall effect was reminiscent of a small but efficient concentration camp. Dougal wondered if the fence was designed to keep people out or to keep them in.

Apart from one window on the ground floor, the rear facade of Campernoyles was as dark as the front. The window was uncurtained and open but protected by vertical bars. Dougal could see nothing but a door flanked by a white oblong, which might be a refrigerator.

The door was opening.

Dougal leapt back to the shelter of the building. Sounds carried easily on the night air: first the chink of glass on glass and then the mumble of lowered voices. As he concentrated on them the volume increased; murmurs became words.

Joe was the first to raise his voice: ". . . and why, for God's sake, did you do it? *Here* of all places. What are they going to think when the van reaches—"

"Nothing. Relax, will you? You just call ahead and tell them not to open that case. Would you rather I'd left him on the premises?"

"But, Alex, you can't go around killing people. Not in this country."

"I just did, old buddy, remember? You Brits are so damn wimpish. You should have done it at once."

"But we don't even know that Bert was a risk. Not for certain."

"Aw, come on. You won't survive very long if you wait for certainties. Be your age. Look, Joe, we can't afford to waste time being sentimental. We've got to be positive. For a start, we need to work out a low profile—"

Vertag's voice stopped as if a pair of scissors had sheared it into silence. Dougal strained to hear a new participant in the conversation.

"Could you check the takings, Joe? I'll lock up." It was Mary. Alcohol had blurred the edges of her voice. Dougal thought he could detect a naked yearning for Joe but realized that he was probably hearing it because he was expecting it to be there.

"Okay. Let the dog out, will you?"

There was a dull screech as the sash window closed. Dougal had begun to move before he was cut off from the conversation.

The dog. His imagination produced a slavering Alsatian that would immediately scent the presence of an intruder in the alley. The dog would throw itself against the wire fence, snarling with blood lust. Once released, it would trail Dougal through Camden Town with the singlemindedness of a terrier after a rat.

Coward. Dougal walked softly down the alley and turned into the main road. He increased his pace to the fastest he could go without actually running. A stitch immediately began to prod his stomach.

He wasn't scared of the dog. After all, no dog was responsible for the death of Fat Bert. The quivering barman should have taken his own advice: *don't join.*

When had Vertag done it? Either before he had come through the front door of Campernoyles complaining about Arthurians in Hackney or just before Dougal had left. Probably the latter. Joe had spent the last half an hour at their table. At one point Vertag had left—"Need a leak, man"—and he'd been away for several minutes. He must have worked fast to find, destroy, and dispose of Bert in so short a time. An efficient little murder.

And the logical extension to that was an efficient little murderer. Dougal recalled a sentence from De Quincey, whose collected works were among the few books available on the *Sally-Anne:* "People begin to see that something more goes to the composition of a fine murder than two blockheads to kill and be killed. . . ."

Dougal turned left at the Chalk Farm tube station,

trying to force his flagging muscles to maintain their pace. Swiss Cottage—Finchley Road—West Hampstead: he wished he could keep his mind on the familiar geography of London.

"Design, gentleman," De Quincey said, "grouping, light and shade, poetry, sentiment, are now deemed indispensable to attempts of this nature. . . ."

Also, in a world where murder was more than a fine art, its practitioners required a motive.

Judging by Bert's unprepossessing appearance, a financial reason for his death was unlikely. Junkies aren't usually rich; if by any chance they are, they don't look like junkies. A crime of passion seemed equally improbable. Dougal was inclined to attribute the murder to fear or revenge. Bert had either offended or threatened Vertag.

Whatever the motive, Vertag's speed of execution—*execution*—would have aroused De Quincey's admiration. And the almost immediate disposal of the crated body suggested careful planning beforehand—a premeditated murder that must have needed cooperation from Joe. It sounded as though Joe was an unknowing accessory before the fact and an unwilling one after it.

Joe was linked to Vertag, but also to Hanbury, ostensibly Vertag's enemy. In that case, why did Hanbury need to bring Dougal into it? Joe could surely have supplied him with information about Vertag's movements. If Hanbury's business with Vertag was legitimate, why should Vertag be worried by Hanbury's hypothetical involvement with the CIA?

The *CIA*, for God's sake!

Dougal reached the conclusion he should have arrived at last night, at the Café Royal. He was being set up for something, and it was time to escape. Bert's murder had acted as the catalyst, for it overcame Dougal's fear of Hanbury with the greater fear of death.

Whatever Malcolm discovered in Rosington, it was better to escape. Better running than dead. Better jailed than dead, if it came to that.

Questions continued to impinge on his mind like darts on a dartboard; but he knew how dangerous the desire to find answers could be. Probably lemmings rushed over the cliff because they were periodically seized by an urge to discover if seawater was as wet as it looked; or perhaps they had doubts about the validity of the theory of gravity.

A lager can had been abandoned on the curb in an invitingly upright position. Dougal broke into a run and gave his thoughts a holiday. *William Dougal to take the place kick.* The can sailed into the center of the Finchley Road and clattered down into the opposite carriageway. The camber of the road rolled it across the traffic lanes until it clanked home in the far gutter. *He'd done it! A stylish conversion by William Dougal.* The echoes bounced between the blank faces of the buildings on either side of the road. When the echoes stopped, he goaded himself into a run. Jogging was so agonizing that it left no time for thinking.

The lower stories of the big house were in darkness. Dougal tripped over one of the plaster cats in the hall, but decided not to turn the light on. Mrs. Moran liked to save electricity. Besides, he could navigate by the faint glow of one of the upstairs lights. He climbed slowly, still panting despite the fact he had walked the last few hundred yards.

Halfway up the first flight he realized that the light upstairs must belong to his own landing. The attic landing only gave access to his own front door. He was sure the light had not been on earlier in the evening—he had left the house before it grew dark.

That suggested he'd had a visitor, who might or might not still be there.

With one hand on the newel post, he thought it out. Most likely someone in the house had called to borrow some sugar or a saucepan. It was just possible that Malcolm had returned. His real fear was that Hanbury was waiting for him.

He told himself it was stupid to get jumpy. The fact that the light was on was a good sign, after all: it implied that his visitor was not trying to conceal his visit.

There was only one way to find out.

Dougal moved softly up the stairs, pausing to listen at every third step.

On the half landing before his front door were two large suitcases he had never seen before. Lying beside them was a book, its title clearly visible from where he stood: *A National Graphics Resource Centre for Libraries in the United Kingdom.*

A movement near Dougal's door—up on the left beyond his line of vision—sent him scurrying back down two steps. The panic returned, together with a craving for a weapon.

A dark shape rose from the landing and masked the feeble glow from the light bulb.

"Hi, sweetheart," said Zelda. "Am I glad to see you!"

CHAPTER 7

Zelda stood in the center of the sitting room and exclaimed that she just loved Dougal's apartment. Was that a genuine Victorian fireplace?

It was. Dougal dumped her cases beside the door.

"You don't *mind* me coming, do you William?" It was not a question to which a polite answer was possible. "This guy laid a standby to London on me and I couldn't resist it. Greece is so sweaty in August."

"How did you know the address?" Dougal was too overwrought to phrase his curiosity in a more roundabout way.

"Malcolm gave it to me, honey. That last night at Yanni's. You wouldn't remember. You were so wrecked you could hardly remember your own name."

Damn Malcolm.

"It's okay me coming, isn't it?" Zelda—her black flesh bursting exuberantly from a red cotton dress—stared down at him. Her forehead was corrugated with worry and her lower lip, which usually turned up in a joyous curve, was trembling slightly. The unaccustomed expression of sorrow on her face made Dougal feel ashamed of himself.

"Yes, of course it is," he said quickly. "I was just. . . surprised to see you. Sit down and I'll get us a drink."

Having said that, he felt better. His personal universe might be fraying at the edges, but there was no need to take his worry out on innocent bystanders. He just hoped that Zelda wouldn't try to seduce him again. Not tonight: at present he lacked the strength either to resist or to succumb.

"I got you some Scotch at Athens airport." Her smile returned, revealing a set of perfectly white teeth. She unzipped her holdall and decorated the top of the drinks cupboard with three bottles of Johnnie Walker Black Label.

Dougal fetched glasses, ice, and a bottle of ginger ale for Zelda. He had hoped that he had jogged away the possibility of a hangover on the way back from Campernoyles; now he wasn't so sure.

"What are you smiling at?" she asked as he came back from the kitchen.

"Just life. You never know what it's going to throw up on your doorstep." Dougal smiled to take the sting, which he hadn't intended, from the words. It would be unfair to blame Zelda when the guilt belonged elsewhere. He should blame himself or Hanbury. Or life itself, the ultimate culprit. He laughed aloud at the absurdity of blaming life for anything. *Where there's life, there's hope.*

"My, I must have cheered you up." There was a gleam in Zelda's brown eyes. "You looked really down when you came in."

As they worked their way into the first bottle of whisky, Dougal held the conversation on Zelda. It was safer that way. He already knew that she lectured on information science at a small university in Virginia and that her employers had granted her an ill-defined sabbatical in Europe, which apparently permitted her to spend her time lounging like a dusky dolphin on Mediterranean beaches.

But now Zelda was talking enthusiastically about the application of marketing principles to the deployment of information resources. "Information is a product, right? You got to sell it. I'm writing a paper on it, and I want to contact this guy in London who's been doing a lot of research in the area. The real problem comes down to feedback evaluation."

Dougal nodded gravely. *Feedback* was a word that always reminded him of a toddler announcing the rejection of his supper.

Zelda laughed. "Don't look like that. I know you think it's bullshit. But it's a way to earn a living. You know what I wanted to do when I was a sophomore? I was going to live in a garret on the Left Bank and write blank verse tragedies about a beautiful black girl starving for her art in Paris."

"And did you?"

"I gave it a couple of months and then I went right back and did a master's in librarianship and information science. I need an institution around me, I guess. And that monthly paycheck." She reached for the whisky. "I'm a kept woman, honey. I have to be. But you can get away with a hell of a lot if you're the token black woman on a liberal-minded faculty."

"Sounds as if you've made a good bargain."

"Yeah. I play the system and usually win. It's just that sometimes—hell, the other guy's steak always looks nicer than the one you got. Are your folks rich or something? How do you manage?"

Dougal replied that he didn't. He tried to explain why it was important to him to stay outside organizations: the more you lived in and for a group, the less your personal autonomy became. It might be true that no man was an island, but it was preferable to be a peninsula rather than a few landlocked acres in the middle of a continent.

He made no attempt to disguise the financial difficulties that such a geographical preference entailed; he stressed it was an emotional choice, not a moral one.

Zelda was a good listener, asking questions and laughing in the right places. The conversation moved away from the particular as the level in the whisky bottle crept down to the halfway mark. Philosophies of life led quite naturally to a discussion of the policies of the President of the United States.

"Sweetheart, the *real* question is whether the President was reared on a bottle or a breast." Zelda crossed one shapely leg over the other and began to giggle.

The question sabotaged the seriousness remaining in the evening. They continued to toss sentences between them, but without any pretense of coherence. Dougal noticed that the room was swaying. He drew this to Zelda's attention. It was not, he said, that uncomfortable movement alcohol sometimes induces, where the stomach swings one way and the rest of the body and the immediate surroundings swing the other. No, this was like a stable and slow-moving roundabout—like the restaurant on top of the Post Office Tower.

"Wow!" said Zelda. "That's beautiful. Rocking to the rhythm of the universe." She held out her glass for a refill.

Dougal was feeling warm and relaxed. He seemed to have walked into an ice age on his return to London. The thaw was due to Zelda. In his mind there formed the thought that it would be brutal to run off tomorrow without a word to her.

"Hey. I have to go away in the morning. You're welcome to stay here if you want." He heard himself add, "Or come too." He wondered if it was just the whisky speaking.

"Where you going?"

"I . . . don't know. Maybe with Malcolm."

"He's kind of weird. One of those macho gays in a delayed adolescence, I guess." She yawned. "Let's go to bed and talk about it in the morning."

She was right about Malcolm, Dougal realized, at least in part. He stood up and held onto the chair back until he got his sea legs. The morning could wait. He proposed to Zelda that one should always keep problems in the future: that way they couldn't infiltrate the present.

Zelda laughed until a hiccup stopped her. She asked Dougal if he wanted to make sweet music together tonight. He declined on the grounds that he was at present out of tune.

Zelda heaved herself to her feet and accepted Dougal's arm into the bedroom. Once there, her legs buckled and she fell on the bed. "You know, I really like you," she said softly. Sleep or stupor abruptly overtook her.

Dougal bundled her feet on the bed, eased off her sandals, and rolled the blanket around her. On impulse, he bent and kissed her. He went back into the sitting room and crawled into Malcolm's evil-smelling sleeping bag.

He lay on his back and stared up at the skylight, a tentlike structure that was a relic of the days when the entire flat had been one large billiard room. The gray, predawn half-light was already struggling through the grimy panes. A bird thudded on to the ridge pole of the wooden frame and chirrupped enthusiastically.

Dougal turned over on his side. Although his hip was grinding into the floor and the bird seemed to be acting as a cheerleader for all its feathered friends from Potter's Bar to Purley, he knew he would have no difficulty in sleeping. Unconsciousness was as inevitable as the swimming pool at the bottom of a water slide.

He should be wondering about the murder at Campernoyles—the details of his flight and even the possibility of an anonymous tip-off to the police.

But his thoughts wanted to take him elsewhere: next door, into the bedroom. He was beginning to regret that he wasn't there in the flesh—on the bed, under the duvet, and beside Zelda.

Saturday morning began sooner than Dougal had anticipated. He woke up at nine feeling refreshed, clear-headed, and extremely hungry. Waking on the floor after too little food, too much whisky, and not much sleep seemed an unexpected regimen for avoiding a hangover. But it had been so successful that he promised himself he would try it again.

He looked in on Zelda. She was still asleep, curled on her side with her thumb in her mouth. The sight of her brought the problems flooding back. The first thing to do was to contact Malcolm, without Zelda being in a position to overhear.

No. Perhaps the first thing was a cup of coffee.

But a series of disappointments was lying in wait for him in the kitchen. Malcolm had used up the last of both the coffee and the muesli. The only tea available was some three-year-old Gunpowder Green that smelled of tuna fish. The milk had been left out overnight and was well on its way to becoming cheese. The refrigerator contained nothing beyond a selection of fungi in delicate shades of green and gray and the sort of smell that made you step back two paces and sneeze.

Dougal scribbled a note for Zelda—*Gone to buy breakfast. Back soon*—and left it on top of her shoulder bag. It would be a good time to ring Malcolm; he would probably be having breakfast himself.

He let himself quietly out of the flat, noticed that once again the postman had forgotten his existence, and walked down to West End Lane. He bought a paper, for the sake of the change, and found a public telephone box that was both working and unoccupied. As the number rang, he stared through the red bars at the sun-filled outside world. It was astonishing: everyone was smiling, even the people in the queue that had already formed outside the call box.

The hotel receptionist grumpily agreed to look for Malcolm. There was a long silence. At one point, the telephone squeaked into Dougal's ear; he quieted it with another coin. He smiled at the queue of three outside the telephone box.

"William." Malcolm's voice sounded thick and irritated. Dougal smugly suspected the presence of a hangover at the other end of the line. "What a bloody awful time to ring. My eggs are going cold."

"Sorry," Dougal said perfunctorily. "Look, the, um, situation's changed." He groped for words that could be trusted to convey his meaning to Malcolm alone. "You were right to doubt our fat friend the other night. His venture's fundamentally unsound. I'm pulling out at once. To be on the safe side, I think perhaps we should take a little holiday."

"You've seen sense at last. What did Hanbury—"

"Later." Dougal tried to telecommunicate the need for discretion. "Have you had any luck with your inquiries yet?"

"Yes. I had to spend quite a lot of your money but—"

"Never mind that. What was the result?"

Malcolm, with infuriating deliberation, refused to reveal the end of his story before he had dealt with its beginning. He described, in some detail, the inky stains left on his hands by back copies of the *Rosington Observer*. He included a few remarks on the dress sense of the youth of the town—"Quite primitive, my dear." Then: "After an hour or two, a definite picture was starting to emerge. About your late lamented friend, I mean. And later last night I was able to confirm it.

66

From the horse's mouth, I met *such* a nice bobby in the bar and we had dinner and. . ."

The pips punctuated the conversation again. Malcolm continued talking through them, evidently unaware that Dougal couldn't hear him.

". . . suicide while the balance of the mind was disturbed, or at least befuddled. It caused quite a stir locally, you know. But not a hint of hanky-panky."

"Good." Dougal pushed the implications out of his mind; they would have to wait until later. "How soon can you be back in London?"

"Early evening," said Malcolm promptly. "I've a lunch date. With my horse."

Dougal thumbed in the last coin he had. The phone box rejected it. No time to argue, cajole, or make barbed comments about Malcolm's sordid amours. "Don't come back to the flat," he said urgently. "Zelda's there, that's why I'm in a call box. Try to get to the Freemasons' Arms in Hampstead by six, okay?"

"Zelda? You mean the black and comely Colossa from Rhodes? I thought—"

The telephone began to emit a continuous whine. Dougal put down the receiver. There were six people waiting outside now; the first in the queue, a Hell's Angel with I LOVE E II R tattooed on his naked chest, was kicking red paint from the kiosk with an immense jackboot.

Dougal emerged and held the door open for him. The Angel unexpectedly said, "Fanks, mate."

The supermarket, even at this time of the morning, was crowded. Dougal grabbed a wire basket and moved slowly up and down its aisles, bouncing off other shoppers. It was as if he had been injected into a pinball machine. He hadn't bothered with a list, of course, so he took items from the shelves as he saw them. Trolleys and baskets attacked him from all angles, but Dougal hardly noticed. His mind was elsewhere.

His initial reaction to Malcolm's news had been a surge of relief. Hanbury had been bluffing; he had no threat to hold over Dougal—nothing substantial, at any rate. Dougal briefly considered the moral obligation conferred by a thousand pounds but decided to discharge himself from it on the grounds that the money was owed to him from the sale of the diamonds; moreover, Hanbury had forfeited any claim to Dougal's loyalty by portraying Vertag as a harmlessly normal member of society. It was difficult to doubt that Hanbury had known Vertag was a killer from the start.

So Dougal could withdraw. It would be wise to lie low for a while, since Hanbury could not be trusted to reach the same conclusion as Dougal had about the rightful ownership of the thousand pounds. Perhaps a month or two in Ireland would be the answer. The thought of damp skies and autumn colors seemed attractive after the harsh light and brash blues of a Mediterranean summer.

And it would be pleasant to see more of Zelda—though not at the flat, because that qualified as a known haunt.

But there was an undercurrent of fear that lent a feverish improbability to these euphoric plans. True, it was partly due to his almost superstitious respect for Hanbury's powers. Another reason for disquiet was that it had been so easy to discover that Hanbury had no real hold over him.

Too easy?

Hanbury must have known that it was only a matter of time before Dougal was able to call his bluff. Therefore time must be the crucial factor in his calculations: Hanbury could have only needed his cooperation for a short while. Dougal might have already accomplished—unwittingly—what Hanbury had intended him to do. Or perhaps Dougal was not going to be allowed to live long enough to withdraw his cooperation.

Now that was ridiculous. *Don't be fanciful,* Dougal told himself. He had permitted relatively rational thought to degenerate into a labyrinth of ill-conceived speculations. Today would seem less of a potential nightmare once it was solidly grounded on a cooked breakfast.

Dougal moved through a checkout point like a component on an assembly line. Once outside on the pavement, he paused to examine his purchases, seeing them clearly for the first time.

Why on earth had he bought a family-size jar of mango chutney? He loathed the stuff.

"Mango chutney," Mrs. Moran said, peering into Dougal's carton of groceries. "How nice. It always reminds me of when my husband and I were in India. Except we spent most of our time in Quetta and Karachi, and they're not in India anymore, are they? It was all red on the map in those days. My husband hated it. Mango chutney, I mean."

Dougal smiled politely and edged toward the stairs.

"I just popped out to say that your uncle was here. I looked out of the window and there he was, closing the front gate. He must have rung your bell and had no reply. You've only just missed him."

Dougal, careless of appearances, turned abruptly and ran up the stairs. He ought never to have left Zelda alone. His mind produced a phantasmagoria of charnel-house imagery: ragged wounds in dark skin, brown eyes looking at nothing, blood on the bed.

He dropped the carton outside his door and wasted precious seconds finding his key and inserting it into the Yale lock. He had left it on the latch when he went down, but now the catch was down.

At last he got the door open and ran through to the bedroom. Its emptiness was almost as shocking as what he had feared might be there.

A few more seconds confirmed that Zelda was gone.

Dougal stood in the center of the sitting room, forcing his breathing back to normal. His first fear had given way to relief, but now a second fear, almost as terrible as the first, was rapidly gaining ground.

At that moment he noticed that the typewriter on the table by the door was no longer empty. A rectangle of paper reared from its dusty interior. He ripped it out and read the few, impeccably typed lines it contained.

On an impulse I called to see why you hadn't telephoned last night. We had—and have—an arrangement. I find I was wise to do so. I've borrowed your little friend as a way of ensuring your continued interest. Not your usual type, I would have said. Don't call me, I'll call you. *A bientôt,* dear boy.

There was no signature; it would have been superfluous. *Not your usual type.* . . . Dougal could imagine Hanbury's reaction to Zelda: the quizzical lift of the eyebrow and the elaborate politeness. Hanbury would be adept at using politeness as a social weapon, his personal napalm developed for front-line use in the class war.

Damn the man! Dougal sat down heavily and resisted the urge to put his head in his hands. On the face of it, Hanbury's motive seemed obvious: he had kidnapped Zelda on the assumption that Dougal was emotionally entangled with her, as a hostage to keep Dougal well behaved. In that case Dougal would be expected to continue his surveillance of Vertag and Campernoyles.

But Hanbury's words, *Don't call me,* hinted at a contradiction: they suggested that he was no longer very interested in Vertag's movements.

Yet why else would he bother with a prisoner?

If the *why* was unsatisfactory, the *how* was even harder to grasp. If Hanbury was somehow aware that Dougal knew Vertag to be capable of murder, it could go some way to explaining the kidnapping of Zelda. In that case, Hanbury must be having his watcher watched: he had set Dougal to watch Vertag, and a third person to watch Dougal.

Who?

Dougal wondered about the improbably polite Hell's Angel. He had certainly been around this morning; he might even have overheard some of Dougal's call to Malcolm; and he could have telephoned Hanbury immediately afterward.

But how could the Angel have eavesdropped last night? Dougal had been unnaturally alert at Campernoyles and even more so in the alley beside it.

Don't call me. . . . Dougal went to the kitchen, poured a glass of water, and drank it in one go. He decided to think about the future on the grounds that it might be easier to grasp than the past. At least his future was—and would always be—his personal property. Until it happened: when it became the present, other people would muscle in and complicate it. People like James Hanbury.

There were three options before him, none of which lacked drawbacks. He could follow his original plan and run away. He could—if he cared enough for Zelda's well-being—go to Campernoyles and put himself under Vertag's orders. Or . . .

Dougal shifted restlessly and faced his reflection in the mirror on the left of the sink. He looked unhealthy and badly in need of a shave. Every time he looked in a mirror, he needed a shave. The mirror itself, whose surface was covered with layers of dust and kitchen grease, did nothing to improve his appearance.

His reflection rippled as it ran over a network of squiggles that straggled along the lefthand edge of the mirror, half hidden by the enamel and rust of the Ascot water heater.

He bent closer, and the squiggles resolved themselves into words: GRAVERS ELMNEY.

CHAPTER 8

Nicholas Marston was a journalist by profession and a trainee rock star by aspiration. He was sitting cross-legged on the grass, studying the two sheets of paper Dougal had given him. His white forehead, growing ever more egglike as the black tide of his hair receded, glistened with sweat. He reached out for his can of lager and the lank curls on either side of his face swung listlessly forward.

He sighed. "I asked you to keep it simple, William."

"I have."

Nick stabbed his index finger reproachfully at Dougal. "We had a deal. Information on Joe Graver in return for two nice easy songs. How can I pass these off as my own compositions to the other guys in the band if I can't even play them?" The finger dive-bombed down to an offending chord shape. "What's *that*, for God's sake?"

"Just an augmented D. I've put the chord diagrams on the back. Like an ordinary D, but you sharpen the A."

Nick grunted and began to read through the lyrics. Dougal nursed his can of lager and stared at the Sunday joggers, dogs, and footballers who were rushing energetically around Hampstead Heath. The continuing fine weather had brought them out in their battalions; he and Nick were lucky to have found this relatively secluded corner near the mixed bathing pond. He wanted to grab the buff folder beside Nick, but knew better than to try to rush things.

Nick took his musical ambitions very seriously and expected others to do the same. Twelve years ago they had played together in the school rock and roll band, an experience that had given Nick an entirely misleading impression of Dougal's musical capabilities. Nick, playing a mediocre rhythm guitar, had fallen victim to the stardust syndrome. He was now an enviably successful freelance journalist, but still his heart's desire was to see his albums riding high in the charts of *Melody Maker* and his name in lights above Wembley Stadium.

"This one's okay." Nick pointed at the song headed "Darling Don't Wanna Play Politics Anymore." " 'SMP's on the Mall again, SPG at the door' and all that stuff about the red flag over the Admiralty and the little urban shits. Yeah, fine. But the other one's a bit, well, existential. 'I go leisurely insane in the room behind my brain, but it's okay.' You know. I've got to think of my *image*."

"Ah." Dougal improvised wildly. "You have to see it in the context of the music. Contrast is the whole point of the song. Reflective lyrics set against a raunchy hip-swiveling twelve-bar. The impact depends on how you sing it. You want to aim midway between early Elvis and middle-period Mick Jagger." He paused to allow the implied compliment to sink in and then abandoned subtlety. "I don't think many people could handle it, but your voice has the right—um—bluesy throatiness."

Nick looked modestly away and began to pick his teeth with a guitar plectrum.

Dougal tossed a cassette onto his lap. "I taped them both last night, to give you an idea of tempo and melody. They're all yours. Absolutely."

Nick remained silent for a moment, doubtless savoring dreams of stardom. Suddenly he smiled at Dougal. "It's a bargain. Let me know if you write any more. Actually, we've got a vacancy for a keyboard player."

Dougal shook his head. "Not now. I'm leaving London for a while." He briefly regretted the necessity. "Tell me, how did you get on with Graver?"

When Dougal had found Zelda's message yesterday morning, he had realized that his three options had contracted to one. He couldn't escape his responsibility for Zelda; and, for reasons that remained obscure to him, he didn't even want to try.

It was difficult to understand how she had learned where she would be taken. The most likely hypothesis was that Hanbury had used the telephone in her presence and mentioned their destination.

GRAVERS ELMNEY. It made sense, of a sort. Joe Graver, the man who was both Hanbury's friend and Vertag's, was somewhere in the middle of this business. Dougal had found Elmney in his road atlas: it was a Gloucestershire village on the edge of the Forest of Dean, close to the Welsh border. Perhaps Graver had a cottage down there, which could be converted into an isolated rural prison.

He had telephoned Nick and arranged for him to do some preliminary legwork. Nick had a genius for quarrying information; and his hunger for new material would ensure that he did the job well. No one could know of his connection with Dougal. Nick himself, in consideration of past and future musical favors, was content to restrain his curiosity about Dougal's motives.

As Nick picked up the file, his manner underwent a transformation. The laid-back embryonic rock star vanished; his spine straightened; and the lager stood forgotten at his elbow.

"I don't know what your interest is in Joe Graver," he began, "but if Elmney comes into it you'll need to know about the whole family. They're a clannish brood. You can look through the file later. That's got photocopies of most of the basic stuff—*Who's Who* entries, Pevesner's remarks on Elmney Castle—"

"Joe Graver owns a *castle?*" Dougal couldn't keep the incredulity from his voice; he found it difficult to imagine anyone less likely than Joe to have a stately home in Gloucestershire.

"Well, not exactly. His father owns it, though it's probably mortgaged." An expression of surprise flitted across Nick's features. "You *have* been kept in ignorance, haven't you? I'd better give you a potted family saga. It starts with John Joseph Graver, who was born in Gloucester in the 1880s. Standard Dick Whittington story: he began as a butcher's apprentice and ended as a landed gent. He got into a tinned meat company and expanded with it in the boom years of the Great War. He married the boss's niece in 1930—Matilda Byfield, who's still alive as the dowager Lady Graver. Johnnie and Matilda inherited the whole concern in thirty-two. That same year they produced a son and heir—Thomas Byfield Graver, who's your Joe's father.

"Johnnie did even better in the next war: he trebled the size of his business and did a stint as lord mayor of London. In those days, that particular rainbow ended in a baronetcy as well as a crock of gold. He bought Elmney Castle and six hundred acres in 1945 to complement the title." Nick grinned. "He was dead in six months, the poor sod."

"Rags to riches?" murmured Dougal. He was wondering why Nick found it necessary to go into so much detail.

Nick glanced up at Dougal. His small bright eyes were disconcertingly intelligent. "You *do* need the background, you know. If by any chance you're planning to go down to Elmney, you'll run into three generations of Gravers."

"What are your sources?" Dougal asked suddenly.

"An old bloke who used to work on the *FT*. Ninety-three and with a phenomenal memory. Then there's a friend who edits one of the local rags. Plus one or two others. You don't need the names. We're talking about the sort of informed speculation that doesn't usually find its way into print."

Dougal grinned. "I'm reproved. Go on."

"Young Thomas was a minor, of course, when his father died. The old man had made his wife the sole trustee. That was a mistake. She started selling the things she ought to have kept and keeping the things she ought to have sold. She developed a taste for seeing her name in the gossip columns. And she started gambling. The upshot was, when Thos turned twenty-one in 1953, the Gravers weren't quite as rich as they had been. Not poor, either, by any means. Just wondering if they really needed two chauffeurs.

"Lady Graver decided it was up to Thos to restore the family fortunes. He married a nice American girl his mother chose for him—all very appropriate, the heiress to a corned beef fortune. But the marriage didn't work out. Thos and Theodora just had time to manage one child, Joe, and then she went back to the States. The Gravers hadn't read the small print in the marriage settlement; Sir Thos has had to maintain her ever since."

Dougal silently conceded that Nick was right to insist on the family background; Joe's mother explained at least some of his American flavor. He asked, "Is Joe in line to get some corned beef money?"

Nick shook his head. "Theodora's family didn't really like her marrying an Englishman. Now her relations don't like Theodora, period. They're a conservative lot, and she offended them by getting involved in civil rights and feminism in the sixties. They've more or less disowned her. And the same applies to Joe."

"Go on about Thos."

"Poor Thos. His mother had him taken on by a firm of merchant bankers and encouraged him to wheel and

78

deal on his own account. By the time Thos had finished, the Gravers had lost the town house and most of the land in Gloucestershire. Lady Graver—the dowager, I mean—contributed her bit, especially when the backgammon craze arrived in the seventies. There was a very ugly incident with a Saudi Arabian in seventy-eight, which nearly got into the papers. She stuck a gun up his nostril and accused him of cheating."

Nick must have sensed Dougal's disbelief, for he added, "That's what I was told. By someone who was there. Everyone who knows the woman says that describing her as eccentric is an understatement. She seems to be Debrett's answer to Buffalo Bill. Thos, by all accounts, is totally incapable of controlling her. They say he lives in a fantasy world now—reading Walter Scott and pacing his battlements. He lists one hobby in his *Who's Who* entry: genealogy. Isn't there a character in one of Disraeli's novels who's a bit like that?"

Dougal's ragbag of a mind obligingly supplied a couple of names: "*Sybil.* Sir Vavasour Firebrace."

"That's it. Firebrace was always trying to revive moribund dignities for himself, wasn't he? Sniffing around his pedigree for dormant peerages and privileges? That's Thos to the life, except Thos hasn't got much of a pedigree to begin with."

Not quite, Dougal thought, though it wasn't worth arguing the point. In the 1840s a peerage brought social prestige and political muscle; nowadays it was more of an encumbrance than anything else. Disraeli's Firebrace pursued antique dignities in the hope of practical present benefits; Thos, on the other hand, must be driven by a need to satisfy some obscurely romantic craving for past grandeur.

"Since Thos failed so spectacularly to be someone in the City," Nick continued, "he's left money matters to his ma. She turned part of the park at Elmney into a market garden in the mid-seventies. It had a shaky start, but it seems to be paying its way now. Though you wouldn't have thought you could run a bungalow on its profit margin. So. You see the circumstances in which Joe grew up: all set to go from clogs to clogs in three generations. But luckily for the Gravers, Joe seems to have inherited a little of his grandfather's financial acumen.

"Not that he showed it at first. He failed his 'A' levels and got caught up in a succession of weird cults, all mildly mystical: witchcraft, reincarnation, paranormal bumps in the night. You know the sort of thing—the usual Aleister Crowley mishmash. Then he got busted. He was dealing in magic mushrooms—psilocybin for school kids. They couldn't get him for that; the mushrooms grow wild along the Welsh borders and they're not even classified as dangerous drugs. But Joe had half a gram of cocaine for his own use, so they did him for possession. He got off with a fine, thanks to the family pulling strings. The trial seemed to sober him up. He started Campernoyles a couple of months later."

"Where did he get the money from?"

"Lady Graver. She's got a soft spot for Joe. He persuaded her to sell what must have been her last movable valuable: a Cotman she'd inherited from her uncle Byfield. It was a shrewd move: Joe opened Campernoyles just as London was ready for wine bars."

"I went there." Dougal felt himself shying away from the memory. "It didn't look particularly prosperous."

"If a wine bar lasts more than twelve months, you can be sure it's prosperous. Besides, it's not just a wine bar. You remember the market garden? Joe handles the marketing of the produce from Campernoyles. And Elmney has diversified into the usual consumer rusticana as well—honey with fancy labels, English soap made from recipes in seventeenth-century herbals. The Gravers may not be making a bomb, but they're a damn sight better off than they were a few years ago."

Dougal remembered the two brand new Campernoyles vans. Joe might be an efficient junior capitalist, but it was still perfectly possible that the legitimate business of Campernoyles was in part a cover for a criminal enterprise.

"Someone in the Graver family isn't devoid of a sense of irony," Nick was saying. "Do you know what a campernoyle is?"

Dougal shook his head.

"It's an archaic word for a mushroom. Same root as *champignon*, I suppose. Joe's problems with mushrooms led to Campernoyles."

Dougal was suddenly, if irrationally, convinced that he knew the source of the name. It had to be Hanbury. Campernoyles belonged to the same family of humor as James F. E. Stuart, the Old Pretender. If Dougal was right, how far back did Hanbury's connection with the Graver family go? He remembered Hanbury's unexpected remark about Joe: "He's a good boy."

"How about Joe's life outside his business interests?" Dougal asked cautiously.

Nick looked sharply at him. "You mean the British Apocalyptic Society, don't you? Don't come the innocent with me: that's what you wanted to know about all along."

Dougal neither affirmed nor denied this. He gave what he hoped was an inscrutable yet receptive smile.

"Joe founded the BAS just after Campernoyles got going. As you know, he'd dabbled in that sort of thing before, without coming down in favor of any particular belief system. Maybe he felt the time had come to make up his mind. In any case, he's stuck to the BAS ever since. I suppose he could have done worse: waiting for the end of the world is more realistic than most of his past activities."

"What do they actually do?"

"Not much. As far as I can see, they just sit about waiting. They've floated one or two schemes—one was for a compulsory course in postapocalyptic survival to be included in the curriculum of all state schools; another tried to interest big business in a chain of privately sponsored fallout shelters; and they have what they call a Research and Development Division, which churns out imaginative fiction under the name of Armageddon Scenario Reports. All hot air: it keeps them warm and happy."

"Has the BAS attracted any official attention?"

Nick's face went blank, as if he'd switched off his expression. "I wouldn't know, would I?"

Dougal swore silently at his own ineptitude. If Nick

had any sort of contact with the Special Branch, he would hardly want to broadcast the fact.

"No, of course not," he said quickly. "I wasn't asking for facts; I just wondered if you had an opinion. Not that it matters."

Nick looked at his watch and scrambled to his feet. "I'm late. I'm meant to be meeting someone for lunch." He picked up the songs and the cassette. "I hope these are worth it."

"I'm sure they will be. I'm working on a couple more; you can have those as well if you want."

"Yeah, why not." Nick turned to go and then hesitated, as if aware he was being rather churlish to someone who might have given him the raw material of stardom. "One of my sources gave me a name you might find useful if you want any more background info on the Graver family. Old stuff, I mean. Apparently he used to be their solicitor until quite recently. He's a chatty old soak who lives in Gloucester. I'm told he usually has a liquid lunch in a pub in Westgate, wherever that is."

"What's his name?"

"I think it was Hanbury. Charles Edward Hanbury."

CHAPTER 9

"You bloody fool," said Malcolm with the deliberation of one whose conclusion sprang from an exhaustive knowledge of his subject. "Ever since you got Hanbury's telegram on Rhodes you've been behaving like a lunatic. In fact, you've been doing it for the last six months. Can't you see how *stupid* you're being? You used to be quite sensible. Now you're like a kid with a wooden sword itching to take on the U. S. Marines and the SAS in one go. Why did you come back when Hanbury called you? Why did you accept his offer? And why the hell are you trying to turn into a knight errant?"

He sat back, breathing heavily. They were in the crowded garden of a Hampstead pub; shrieking toddlers maneuvered like berserk Dodgems among the crisp packets and dog turds.

One infant in denim dungarees pointed at Malcolm. "Look, mummy. That bugger over there has gone all red."

"Hush, darling," fluted his mother. "Don't point. It's not nice."

Malcolm scowled at the child with such ferocity that he burst into tears. He switched his aggression back to Dougal: "Well?"

Dougal made a gallant effort to evade the question by suggesting that only in fairy stories did people have convincing motives. Malcolm was not satisfied and probed further.

"We came back from Rhodes because we were bored there," Dougal said at last. "Because we needed money and there was a chance Hanbury would provide some. And, if you must know, I wanted to find out what had happened to Amanda."

Malcolm snorted with derision. "You're a closet romantic. Next one."

"You know the answer to that. Hanbury was blackmailing me."

"He also gave you a thousand quid. You could have vanished."

Dougal shrugged and eyed Malcolm's rolling tobacco. "In the short term it seemed wiser to play along while you checked his story. Come on, it was perfectly reasonable."

"Suicidal, you mean. If you meet a predator in the jungle you run away; you don't hang about and ask him what he's doing there."

"Sometimes you get tired of running away. I can't spend the rest of my life giving Hanbury the right of way."

"Your life won't last very long if you don't. Look,

William, I know what I'm talking about here; you don't."

"In the end, we're talking about me. I used to think—"

"It's that woman." Malcolm ran his fingers violently through his hair. "Your maiden in her dolorous tower. God, you hardly know her. Have you even—?"

Dougal shook his head.

"Well, there you are. You're under no obligation to her. You're not in love with her. She's like someone who gets involved in a motorway pileup through no fault of her own: it's very sad, but there's nothing you can do about it. Now, the sensible thing to do is to forget all that"—Malcolm gestured toward the buff folder that Nick had given to Dougal—"and piss off abroad. I'll come with you. Take the money and forget it all."

"It wouldn't work. She got involved because of me, and I'm not quite callous enough to be able to leave her to Hanbury and his friends." Dougal knew there was more to it than this. Zelda had brought him warmth and reassurance, as well as whisky, at a time when he had badly needed all three. "Besides, I'm not going to do anything stupid. I'll go down to Elmney; they won't be expecting me; if I can't get her out, I'm not going to make a martyr of myself."

"Why not tip off the police? Anonymously, of course. Do the grunters good to have something useful to do."

"What would I tell them? That someone I can't prove I know has been kidnapped for a reason I'd rather not mention by a man called Hanbury of no fixed address. Then I say she's imprisoned in the home of an eminent Gloucestershire baronet who also happens to be a JP and on the local police board. Hell, it would be the sort of call that they giggle about in the police canteen. The most they would do would be to ring Sir Thomas and have a man-to-man chuckle about it. And that would warn the Gravers and Hanbury. Damn it, she may not even be at the castle."

Dougal abruptly stopped. He was aware that his voice had grown louder. Perhaps Zelda's message had really been written by Hanbury. He shook his head vehemently: that way lay madness.

"Okay, calm down." Malcolm's voice was unusually gentle. "Did you get much out of your journalist friend this morning?"

Dougal nodded. "Were you able to get me a car?"

Malcolm pulled a set of keys from his jeans. "It's a van actually. An Escort. I hired it for a week. It set you back a bob or two: Nobby's an old mate, but he never lets personalities get in the way of his profit margins."

"Has he got a garage?" Dougal asked idly.

"Sort of. He's really a theatrical costumier, but if you got the money he'll get you anything, on or off the stage. While I was there I also bought something from him. Here." He picked up a white plastic carrier bag beside his feet and passed it along the bench to Dougal. "No, don't flash it around. Keep it in the bag while you look."

The bag was surprisingly heavy. Something hard was wrapped in an oil-stained rag that had once been

87

a pillowcase. Dougal fumbled with the folds of the cloth and found himself facing the dark snout of a revolver.

"It's an old Webley, standard officer's issue. Probably fell off the back of a lorry in 1945, but it's in very good nick. There are twelve rounds in the bottom of the bag. You'd better call it Excalibur."

Dougal recognized the make: it was the kind of gun his father would have worn to war. He was aware of a sour taste in his mouth, and of the fleeting thought that there was a lot to be said for pacifism. He pushed the bag back to Malcolm. "I don't want it."

"You're not having it. I am."

"But you're going abroad, aren't you?"

Malcolm grinned. "I hoped we both were. But I don't think you're safe on your own. Besides, Hanbury's an arsehole."

As Malcolm negotiated the van among the Sunday afternoon traffic on the A40, Dougal told him what Nick had discovered. The van was nine years old and had been repainted the color of French mustard; the job had been done inexpertly by hand, so the texture of the paintwork reinforced the illusion.

But there was nothing wrong with the engine. Once they reached the motorway section, Malcolm settled down to a steady seventy-five. After a while the conversation died; Dougal began to flick through the contents of the buff folder.

Much of the material duplicated, or supplied unnecessary detail to, Nick's verbal appraisal of the Gravers. The sheer quantity of notes and photocopies surprised

Dougal; it demonstrated the extent of Nick's need for songs he could call his own.

The last six sheets, held together by a separate staple, dealt with the castle itself. Dougal read them avidly; it had suddenly occurred to him, not before time, that the physical layout of the place was just as important as the background of its inhabitants. There were several pages from a book called *Lesser Strongholds of the Western Marches*, published in 1909. The first castle at Elmney had been a Norman motte-and-bailey earthwork. Its main purpose was to serve as a link between Monmouth in the south and Goodrich to the north.

For some generations the castle had been part of the vast possessions of the de Clare family. At other times in the Middle Ages it was held directly for the crown. A twelfth-century de Clare had built a curtain wall of stone around the bailey and leveled the motte, which was already, owing to the lie of the land, showing signs of slipping into the Wye. A few years later, the wall was strengthened with four square towers and a gatehouse. Edward I transformed this gatehouse in the first years of his reign: the two semicircular bastions with linked upper stories effectively formed a miniature keep; the writer believed this to be roughly contemporary with—and perhaps even the prototype for— the far grander keep gatehouse that dominates the sophisticated defenses of Caerphilly Castle.

No trace was now left of the buildings within the curtain, but the writer speculated wistfully about the positions of the hall, solar, chapel, and kitchens. Dougal wondered if they had ever existed in stone: soon after the building of the new gatehouse, Wales had been subdued, thereby nullifying Elmney's strategic importance; no one would have wasted money on a redundant stronghold.

The castle achieved a brief and inglorious prominence during the Wars of the Roses. Polydore Vergil's *Anglica Historia* mentioned that it changed hands three times within a single week. Dougal felt a surge of irrational optimism as he read this. The information suggested that Elmney was difficult to defend; though Dougal lacked the advantage of an army and its attendant siege train, at least he was free to believe that history was on his side.

Henry VIII granted the castle to an ambitious merchant of Monmouth. The new owner gutted it and erected a Tudor mansion within the shell of the curtain walls and towers. He punched great windows through the medieval masonry and allowed the castle walls beyond his new house to fall into disrepair. His great-grandson, the writer remarked, doubtless regretted the alterations: he declared for the king in 1642; six years later, the castle's defenses were systematically slighted by a detachment of the New Model Army.

The sack of the castle brought Elmney's fortunes to their lowest ebb. The historian's prose slipped into elegaic overdrive as he dealt with this period: "Elmney, once the valued possession of kings and earls, ceased to be the residence of gentlefolk. That part of the mansion which remained habitable was leased to a local farmer who permitted a stonemason to plunder the ruins; the stately habitation of antiquity fell victim to banausic greed; the rude grunting of swine filled a courtyard which had once resounded with the clarions of chivalry. . . ."

Fortunately Gothic architecture ceased to be a liability by the end of the eighteenth century and instead became picturesque. A distant relative of Lord Byron bought both castle and estate. His family was responsible for the laying out of the park and the restoration of the building.

Dougal turned to the plan. It showed that the castle was on the tip of a tongue of land that protruded into the Wye Valley. The park was to the south; it was shaped like a segment of an imaginary circle, with the castle at the circle's notional center. The gatehouse stood in the middle of the south front; the Tudor house extended between it and the southwest tower. The nineteenth-century renovators had added a wing that linked the gatehouse to the southeast tower, with the result that the present house was an irregular oblong backing against the entire length of the south curtain wall.

The east and west walls were shorter than the south and sloped inward. The north wall was shorter still. The castle looked like a broad-based isosceles triangle whose apex had been amputated. It was clear from the relative sizes of walls and towers that the builders of the castle had designed it according to the geography of the site: the lie of the land must encourage a besieging force to approach from the south.

The northern fortifications between the house and the river were, according to the writer, "much ruined." In many places the curtain wall had vanished altogether, though Colonel Smith-Pryce's excavation of 1896 had uncovered the foundations of the missing portions.

At this juncture, *Lesser Strongholds of the Western Marches* moved on to Saint Briavel's castle. Dougal turned to the next photocopy and quickly absorbed what Pevesner had to say about Elmney's architecture: a trace of Roman brickwork, removed from elsewhere, could be seen in the undercroft of the southwest tower; the long gallery had been restored and remodeled by Sir Giles Gilbert Scott in a manner that could only be described as unfortunate.

The last sheet had been taken from a map—two and a half inches to the mile Ordnance Survey, by the look of it. The castle was about three miles from Symonds Yat at a point where the Wye briefly ran from east to west. Elmney village was two miles south of the castle, on a B road that wriggled around the hills and eventually joined an A road that crossed the Wye at Monmouth. With the exception of the park, the entire promontory was heavily wooded. The castle straddled the two-hundred-feet-above-sea-level line; to the north the ground dropped sharply down to the river; to the south it sloped gently up into the forest.

Two drives led across the park to the castle; both were turnings off the B road. Between them, on the other side of the road, a picnic spot and a car park had been etched out of the forest. They could leave the van there; at this time of year they would merge with the tourists.

He lifted the map to study it more closely. His hands

were shaking in a way that had nothing to do with the vibration of their journey.

I'm terrified.

Dougal stared out the window. They were passing through one of those Cotswold villages that history, with remarkable foresight, had provided for retired professional people in the twentieth century. Every detail in the scene clamored for his attention. The yellow stone of the cottages and the crisply painted gables of the Tudor inns belonged not in England but in paradise.

"Malcolm?" said Dougal hesitantly. The problem with sharing second thoughts was that they invariably seemed shabbier than the first ones.

"Screw you!" said Malcolm at precisely the same instant, as he braked sharply to avoid a Morris 1100 that emerged from a side road with no thought for the convenience of the oncoming traffic. "Bloody weekend driver. He could have wiped out all his horrible kids. Pity." Malcolm accelerated past the Morris and spent a happy moment baiting its driver by spurting ahead and then braking sharply. "Road hog."

"I've been thinking," Malcolm continued in a quieter voice as they left the village behind. "I'm quite glad you want to make a fool of yourself. I haven't had any excitement since I got busted. Over a year."

Dougal looked at him curiously. "You *like* it?"

"Yeah." Malcolm shrugged. "Maybe *like* is the wrong word. A few risks make you notice you're alive. Make you want to stay alive. You remember that bloke who tried to doublecross me in Berlin last year?"

Dougal nodded. His memory was all too clear on the subject. Malcolm had mentioned the incident one drunken evening on the *Sally-Anne*, on the way to Rhodes. Malcolm had been delivering sixty grams of amphetamine sulphate to a nightclub. The manager, a miniskirted transvestite with the build of a Prussian guardsman, had produced a gun rather than the agreed payment. Malcolm had shot him with the same gun and decamped with the takings from the office safe.

"I've never felt more *real* than I did on that night. Amazing. And the feeling stayed with me for days." Malcolm relapsed into silence.

If that was reality, Dougal thought, he'd rather be fictional.

CHAPTER 10

I am a soldier, Dougal thought, *and this is a military operation. Complete with artillery.*

He wished his father were here: a retired regular army officer would have his uses at present. It was entirely fitting that the origins of Dougal's adolescent rebellion against his father had included a particularly violent argument about pacifism. He would know exactly how to reconnoiter and infiltrate a strong point. After all, he had acquired an MC doing much the same sort of thing in Italy.

Malcolm left the A40 a few miles after Gloucester. Farmland rapidly gave way to forest. The road contracted to a shimmering black ribbon that entangled itself among tree-covered hills and valleys. They were forced to cut their speed—partly because of the contortions of the road but more because everyone else using it was in no hurry. Cars drove sedately down the center of the road at thirty miles per hour, while sheep left the forest to sun themselves on the open tarmac.

The pines rippled like corn; in the distance they

were mottled with purple and looked as soft as a pile of feathers.

Dougal wished he was a camera and could point himself at them forever.

"I could do with a drink," Malcolm said. "We'll crack a tube when we reach the car park. Watch out for an Elmney sign on the left."

Dougal saw the sign almost at once. A white van was emerging from the turning. As Malcolm slowed, its twin appeared behind it.

CAMPERNOYLES FRUIT & VEGETABLES.

"So that part of Nick's story was true," Malcolm said, watching the vans grow smaller in his rear mirror. "Presumably the two you saw on Friday night. Collecting produce from the Gravers' market garden."

"They were delivering something to Elmney as well."

"Fat Bert?"

"Yes. But Vertag said something about other cases besides the one with Bert in. I wonder what was in them."

Malcolm honked at a sheep. "Maybe nothing," he suggested. "They could have been taking back empties."

The forest on the right was suddenly replaced by a stone wall, six feet high and topped with glass.

"Slow down," Dougal said. "That'll be the park. The car park should be on the left in about two hundred yards."

He strained his eyes as they passed a gateway: it stood beside a shuttered lodge that had lost a third of its roof; the gates themselves were of rusted iron; the drive beyond looked overgrown. It was impossible to glimpse the castle, or even the park, because the drive ran obliquely into a belt of trees.

Malcolm signaled left and slowed down. The car park was a graveled rectangle hidden from the road by a bank encrusted with saplings. "Oaks and rowans," Malcolm said.

There were half a dozen cars already there. On one side of the car park was a clear green space bisected by a stream, which the Forestry Commission had evidently designated as a picnic area; there were wooden benches and rough stone hearths, plus a generous supply of litter bins. One family was already settling down to a barbecue; screaming children chased one another among the trees; infants wailed; a transistor was broadcasting "this week's top forty on Radio One!"

"This is perfect," Dougal said.

Malcolm switched off the engine. "As cover?"

"Partly." Dougal had in fact been thinking of another order of perfection.

Malcolm stretched behind his seat and picked up his jacket and the carrier bag. Dougal reached for the cans of lager, which were wrapped in most of this morning's *Observer* to keep them cold. For the first time he noticed a flat box of gray cardboard that had been covered by Malcolm's jacket.

"What's that?"

"Oh, that's Nobby's." Malcolm rolled up his window and yanked open the door. "Shows he must trust me, leaving his stuff in the van. Nice to have friends, eh?"

97

They locked the van and walked a little way into the forest. They sat down in the shade of a beech tree, with the carrier bag between them.

"Time for a spot of briefing," said Malcolm in the voice of one who commands a tank and belongs to a cavalry regiment.

"Shut up, will you?" Dougal was again studying the map. He had the illusion that he was seeing the area through eleventh-century eyes. It was a stupid place to build a castle—perhaps the forest had forced the builders away from the higher ground. Since he had started looking at the castle as an attacker, he had lost both his indecision and most of his fear.

"Okay." Dougal picked up a twig and pointed at the map. "First, we don't know for sure that Zelda's there. Nor who else is at the castle. Thos and his mother. Possibly Joe and Hanbury. Perhaps Vertag. There may be staff inside, and there may be people employed on the estate or in the Campernoyles market garden. But it's unlikely that employees would be too deeply involved. Our main advantage is that they won't be expecting us. I think we should take a look round while the light lasts. You see the forest goes right round the park? There's even a strip to the north between the castle and the river. Lots of footpaths. We could keep to the forest but try to get a good idea of the layout of the park and castle. The whole place is designed on the assumption that people will approach from the south. So, when it gets dark, we could move in from the north. Plenty of gaps in that curtain wall."

"Quite the generalissimo, aren't we? I suppose we take the place by storm and put the garrison to the sword."

Dougal grinned. "No. We just get into the house and find Zelda."

"And if we can't?"

"Well . . . we could always find someone else. Hanbury or Graver for choice. Open negotiations with a hostage to support our case. Standard terrorist tactic, I understand. How do you like it?"

"Dear God. I think it's bloody anachronistic. That girl's turned you into one of your fighting ancestors. Evolution in reverse. Baboons have similar behavior patterns."

"It's curiously liberating, you know." Dougal tried to turn the conversation away from the personal. "Didn't Sartre say he felt freest in the war? Danger somehow—"

"Crap." Malcolm began to paw at the oily bundle in his plastic bag. "Danger just locks you in the present. An exciting prison." There was a click as he fed the first round into the chamber of the Webley. "Stuff Sartre."

Dougal put a blade of grass in his mouth and tried very hard to convince himself that it was a cigarette. "What do you think of the plan?"

Malcolm shrugged. "As good as we can hope for. I leave the tactics to you. I'll just make sure you don't do anything stupid. Have you thought about afterward? I mean, what do we do with Zelda when and if we find her? She's not exactly inconspicuous."

"Vanish for a while. Try to persuade Zelda that she's safer in America."

"You're not going to want to spend the rest of your lives together?"

"No, of course not. I don't know." Dougal scrambled to his feet. "What a bloody silly question."

"I was only asking."

Dougal felt the warm gush of anger subside. "Come on. Let's stop talking and start doing."

It was hard to imagine being with Zelda again. Or not being with her. But he was certain that he didn't want the choice to be made on behalf of both of them by James Hanbury.

The road along the park wall smelled of tar and incontinent sheep. Dougal and Malcolm separated, once they had synchronized their watches with military precision.

Dougal had given himself the western flank. He walked quickly along the grass verge beside the wall, his senses at full stretch. In less than a mile, the wall gave way to a fence that guarded a plantation of conifers. He slipped through the barbed wire and found himself in a green, pine-scented twilight. He knew that a ride slashed through the forest a few hundred yards to his left, but that would take him too far from the park boundary.

Movement was slow and noisy. Dougal tripped over a root and sprawled in a ragged hole left by the uprooting of a tree. His ankle protested vigorously.

Dougal forced himself to remain still. The last thing he wanted was a twisted ankle. The forest was no longer cool and refreshing; it was a sinister cavern, littered with hidden menaces.

To continue through the forest itself would take too much time and was possibly dangerous. The ride would be no use for reconnaissance.

He picked himself up and moved cautiously to the east, toward the park itself. He would make better going on the fringe of the trees and see far more.

It would also increase the chance of someone seeing him.

A trim fence of wire mesh separated the plantation from the park. A ribbon of clear ground, perhaps eighteen inches wide, ran inside the fence. Its regularity suggested that someone had gone methodically crazy with an extremely powerful lawn mower.

Which didn't like thistles.

Distant baas enlightened Dougal. The sheep must make a habit of poking their heads and necks through the fence from the park, on the assumption that the barrier must exclude them from a particularly desirable range of edible delicacies. The swath of grass was the frontier of their foraging.

It was ideal. He could move swiftly with a good range of vision; the forest on his left offered both cover and an escape route. He glanced down at his clothes and congratulated himself on his instinctive choice of colors: brown boots and corduroy trousers, and a faded khaki drill shirt that had once belonged to his father. The sun was now on his left, which would add to the difficulties of a hypothetical watcher on his right.

The park looked unkempt, its meadows studded with rusting agricultural machinery. There were gaps in the avenue of trees that led in the direction of the castle. At a guess, a nineteenth-century owner had imported a landscape gardener, but now neglect held sway. Art had expelled nature; nature's revenge was equally brutal and far more insidious.

An ornamental lake came into view. Its waters were scum-covered and ringed with reeds. Dougal could just make out a water-logged punt nuzzling the rotting jetty.

At the far end of the lake—more of an overgrown pond, really—was a low, probably artificial knoll, topped by a whitewashed summerhouse in the shape of a miniature temple.

For one hallucinatory second, Dougal could see a Regency family taking tea in the shade of the portico, with the lake blue and sparkling below them. The cries of children on the jetty . . .

The present surged back. The whitewash was gray and blotched with damp. The weather had eaten into one of the Corinthian pillars, exposing the plebeian brick beneath. The only cries were those of seagulls, straying inland from the Severn estuary. The present occupants of the castle couldn't afford to maintain Arcadia.

If the Gravers were unable to remedy this landscaped desolation, perhaps they felt a grudge toward Hanbury and Vertag. It was a possibility that might be worth investigation. A crack in the alliance could be exploited.

Dougal's eyes returned to the summerhouse. It should command a view of the south front of the castle. And vice versa.

He stood perfectly still for two minutes, timed on his watch. The only movement in the park came from the sheep in an enclosure on the other side of the avenue. They would be too far away to notice him and betray his presence by their agitation. The Elmney market garden must lie on the other side of the park. The forest behind him was quiet.

The fence bent beneath his weight. It swayed to and fro; the fence posts creaked alarmingly. Dougal tumbled headfirst into the park and swore.

He ran along the perimeter of the lake. The slope of the knoll was steeper than he had anticipated, and several times he stumbled. Dougal's breathing tore savagely at his chest.

After half an hour in the forest, he was unprepared for the openness of the position. He felt naked without trees. Panic, as well as prudence, made him duck into the shelter of the temple.

The portico formed the fourth side of a deeply recessed room. A stone bench, still with two moldering cushions on it, ran round the three walls. The stone-flagged floor was littered with the droppings of birds and sheep.

No one had taken tea here for a very long time.

There was a small window set in the far wall, its glass obscured with grime and cobwebs. Dougal used the palm of his hand to clean a corner of the pane.

The castle was no more than two hundred yards away. He was far too close for safety, but he might as well make the most of it.

The stone of the castle had a reddish tinge, which

glowed a dull orange where the evening sun struck it. The frontage was still the main line of defense of a medieval castle, despite the great Tudor windows and the graveled sweep where once the ditch had been. All the windows on the ground floor were heavily barred: storerooms and household offices, perhaps. Many of the mullioned windows on the first floor were open, but their sills must be at least fifteen feet above the ground. Someone had recently treated the western range to some new slates; but the eastern, Victorian wing looked almost as derelict as the summerhouse. The gates at the center of the facade were open.

Besides the sheep, the only sign of movement came from the top of the gatehouse. The light breeze was flapping a flag against its pole.

Dougal chuckled. So Sir Thos was definitely in residence and determined to demonstrate his baronial pretentions to any low-flying aircraft that might happen to pass.

The wind suddenly flipped the standard out to its fullest extent. Dougal's chuckle became a laugh.

Or, three chevrons gules.

Dougal's mind attracted random facts with the impartiality of flypaper. An old fact collided with a new fact. For the first time, Thos Graver came into focus.

Nick's information had told him that Graver loved speculative genealogy, and that the castle had at one time belonged to the de Clare family. Dougal's knowledge of heraldry was based on a brief teenage obsession. But he knew enough to recognize that Graver was using the arms of Clare as his personal standard—three red chevrons on a gold background.

He quarried his memory for detail. The male line of the de Clares had disappeared at some point in the Middle Ages. Some people would still be able to trace a descent on the distaff side, but none of these would be entitled to use the Clare arms by themselves. If one of the Gravers had deliberately chosen the arms of Clare, the College of Arms would have insisted that they were different from the original. Besides, Graver should display some sign of his baronetcy; Dougal was almost sure that the Red Hand of Ulster should be somewhere on that flag.

The discovery might indicate little more than a sentimental attachment on Graver's part to the former owners of his home. Dougal was certain, however, that there was more to it than this. If Graver was as dedicated to his pedigree as Nick had suggested, he would treat heraldry, genealogy's sister science, with equal respect. He would never dream of flying a standard that wasn't his own.

Unless he believed it belonged to him. Unless he had dreamed himself into self-delusion.

Dougal slumped back on the stone bench of the summerhouse. Martin Luther King had a dream: why shouldn't Graver? If Graver believed he was really the heir to the lands and titles of the de Clare family, wrongly denied to him by the twentieth century, he might well feel no scruples about receiving tax-free payments from Vertag and Hanbury; after all, his dream would make it imperative to maintain his position here at Elmney. A de Clare would not desert his last ancestral possession, even if his name was Graver.

Dougal stretched himself and moved toward the portico. It was time to be gone. He hoped that the northern approach would be more accessible to the passing stranger.

Yap! Yap!

Events began to move with a rapidity that left no time for reflection. Two sheepdogs were streaking up the knoll toward him.

Dougal was fond of dogs, but sheepdogs who felt one was violating a territorial restriction couldn't be depended upon to return the affection.

Flight was clearly out of the question: it would only encourage them to treat him as an alien, two-legged sheep in need of immediate disciplinary action.

He stood still, hands thrust in his pockets and adrenaline pumping through his veins.

The dogs ran up to him, circled their quarry, and began to bark. One of them, its ears laid back against its skull, darted toward him and nipped his thigh.

He reacted without thinking. The need for secrecy was consumed by an emotion that was entirely primitive. The pain was insignificant, but his anger was not. Dougal bellowed without words and advanced on his attacker. The dog, still snarling, retreated.

"Johnny! Clara!"

The heads of both dogs twitched, as if tugged by invisible wires. Their excitement dropped away from them, leaving intimations of guilt behind. They withdrew from Dougal with caution; diplomacy might require a tactical retreat, but the intruder was still potentially dangerous.

"Come *here.*"

The owner of the voice appeared on the slope of the hill. The man had a complexion like a withered Cox's Orange Pippin. He could have been any age between forty and eighty. A black three-piece suit, its material wrinkled and stained, hung from his tall, gaunt figure. Most of the buttons were missing. Beneath the waistcoat was a grubby vest, but no shirt.

The man stopped five yards away from Dougal. The dogs immediately moved to positions just behind him. He ignored them, first fiddling with an egg stain on the lapel of his jacket and then scratching the gray stubble on his chin.

"Didn't bite you, did he?"

Dougal rubbed his thigh. "Just a nip. I don't think he broke the skin."

"Oh, dear," the man remarked unexpectedly. "It's private land, but he still shouldn't have bit you. He had distemper real bad, you see. When he was a pup. Thought he'd die, I did."

"He seems alive enough to me."

"Ah." The man returned to the egg stain. "He's never been quite right in the head since. Oh, he's all right with me and the sheep, but sometimes he goes a bit strange. Sees red. Don't like people he don't know."

"That's okay. No harm done. I shouldn't have been here in the first place."

Conciliation and a swift withdrawal were necessary. It was perhaps fortunate that the dog had bitten him. Dougal was in the wrong as a trespasser, but Johnny's bite had given him a weapon. No shepherd would wish to lose a fully trained dog; if Dougal made a formal complaint, the animal might be at risk. There was no sign that the man had recently been put on his guard against strangers.

But the shepherd seemed to feel that the formalities had not been concluded. He assumed that Dougal would wish to know the full history of the ancestry and upbringing of Johnny. ("Clara's his mother. Wouldn't think it, would you?") The narrative was also designed to impress upon Dougal that none of this would have happened if he had kept off private land.

Dougal pulled the photocopy of the map from his pocket. He knew from experience that possession of a map conferred a harmless idiocy on its bearer. It meant that he was a peripatetic townie with a mysterious desire to wander over the land of strangers. More to be pitied than blamed.

"I was sure there was a footpath near here."

"That's been closed for years. Long before the war. That map's behind the times. You from London?"

Dougal nodded.

"Ah." The shepherd looked pleased to hear his suspicions confirmed. "I went there once. To see the exhibition. We went on the underground and the wife got thrown off one of those escalators. Broke her leg. Shocking. She had to spend a fortnight in hospital. We never went back."

As the shepherd drawled on, Dougal tried to suppress his impatience. He couldn't afford to rush off—the last thing he wanted was any sort of disturbance that might filter back to the shepherd's employers at the castle. It was one of those stupid situations where an urgent desire was shackled by a delicate social necessity.

The old man moved gradually from his autobiography to the subject of country life. He recalled that he used to have to walk ten miles a day "before old Sir John give us a house on the estate." This reminded him that Dougal was on foot.

"You'll be wanting the river," he observed. "All the visitors do. Best way is through the forest. There's a ride through the forest, straight as an arrow. Used to be lovely before they planted those bloody conifers."

The shepherd spat for emphasis.

"How do I reach it?"

"I'll show you. Gate in the fence. Carry on up the path and it hits the ride."

They walked down the knoll toward the forest. The dogs circled them, still keeping a wary distance from Dougal. The western end of the castle slid into view. Dougal paused to do up his perfectly tied shoelace, using the maneuver to cover his movement to the left side of his guide; it was an almost superstitious attempt to screen himself from unseen eyes behind blank windows.

"You on a walking holiday?"

Dougal had no time to reply. Johnny barked, his ears flat against his narrow skull. He ran round the knoll to their right. Clara followed, though with less urgency.

109

"Come *here!*" The shepherd rubbed his chin. "Bloody dog." He set off in pursuit.

Dougal saw him raise his hand in greeting. The dogs must have found another human quarry.

"Afternoon, Mr. Joseph. Didn't bite you, did he?"

CHAPTER **11**

Sir Thomas Graver, Bt., shot to his feet like a startled genie summoned by an imperious master. He had been sitting at a table in the bay window at the far end of the library. The table was littered with papers and with piles of sturdy reference books. In his haste he jolted a corner of the table, precipitating one of the piles on to the floor.

He stared at Dougal, his eyes widening, and backed farther into the window embrasure.

Joe jabbed the barrel of the .22 rifle into the small of Dougal's back. "Face the fireplace. Put your hands on the mantelpiece."

"Who—?" Graver asked. "Is it, um—?"

"It's William Dougal, all right." Joe sounded almost as nervous as his father. "He was snooping round the temple, trying to chat up Jess. Come on, we've got to search him."

Dougal leaned against the mantelpiece, his feet apart, and stared at the picture above it. The arms of Clare, again, this time surmounted by an earl's coronet. The glass in the frame dully reflected the room behind him.

Graver now had the rifle, which he was pointing in the general direction of Dougal's head. The barrel was wavering, but it would be hard to miss at four yards' range, even with a .22. And a .22 bullet in the brain would kill you just as efficiently as one of a larger caliber.

Joe ran his hands from Dougal's ankles up to his armpits. He found a set of keys, a piece of lavatory paper that Dougal was using as a handkerchief, and his penknife. It was not an efficient search, for Joe missed the pockets in Dougal's shirt, which contained his money and the map.

"What now?" Graver asked.

"Why not offer me a chair?" Dougal half turned his head. "If you put me in that big armchair, it would take me about five minutes to get out of it."

"He's right, Pa. Go on."

The armchair was unexpectedly hard and slightly dusty. Dougal sat back in it, stretched out his legs, and crossed his ankles. The panic that had gripped him ten minutes ago was receding, partly because the Gravers were so obviously nervous. They were treating him like an unexploded bomb before the disposal team arrived.

The best policy was to look as relaxed as possible. It was a kind of human poker: two men on their feet, one armed, easily outranked one man lolling in a chair; but his response could turn their very strength into a weakness.

Dougal ignored the men and concentrated on the room. Three sides were paneled in dark-stained Victorian pine; the shelves recessed into the walls mainly contained rows of calfbound volumes whose dusty regularity suggested books bought by the yard. The park stretched beyond the window in the south wall. He could just see the temple over Graver's shoulder.

Joe took the gun from his father and sheltered it behind the armchair on the other side of the fireplace.

Sir Thomas was looking at Dougal, but quickly turned away when his guest caught his eye. He was a small, skinny man with rounded shoulders. Half-moon glasses sat on his bony nose. His wrinkled linen jacket and gray Oxford bags seemed a couple of sizes too large for him.

"What did you tell Jess?"

"Nothing. I played it very cool. Just offered to show our visitor the shortcut to the river and the gun did the rest. Jess thought I was going out after rabbits."

Sir Thomas armed himself with a heavy glass paperweight. He swallowed. "Why are you here? How did you know where to come?"

Dougal stirred in his chair. "The address is in *Who's Who*, you know. I came to collect Zelda."

A plan was shaping itself in his mind. He had to keep Malcolm's presence to himself. Vertag and Hanbury were dangerous unknown quantities, but it looked as if they weren't on the premises; otherwise the Gravers would surely have notified them of his arrival. His hosts at present were scared—of him? It seemed probable that they were even more ill at ease in the world of professional crime than Dougal himself.

Divide and rule.

"Surely," Dougal continued, "James must have told

you to expect me. It's all been *arranged.*"

The emphasis on the last word achieved the desired effect: mystification.

Graver and Joe gave each other looks that would have been speaking if either of them had known what to say.

"It's a con—"

"What has been arranged?"

"I assumed James would have told you. I'd better leave it to him. May I see Zelda now?"

Joe moved a step nearer and poked the rifle in Dougal's direction. "We know who you are," he announced ominously, "and if you think we're—"

"I know who I am too. Aren't you being rather melodramatic? If I had anything nefarious in mind, I'd hardly be wandering around your park in broad daylight, chatting to one of your employees."

Sir Thomas put the paperweight down on his table. "This whole business has been grossly mismanaged. Mr. Dougal, you will appreciate that we are all in a very difficult position. One cannot be too careful."

"Quite." Dougal, drunk with fear, erected his fingers into a steeple to minimize their trembling. "Your mistake," he conceded generously, "was entirely understandable. I should have telephoned beforehand." He had to buy time before the conversation got out of control. "Tell me, are you descended from the Clares? I noticed your standard."

Graver blushed. The years were stripped away from him and he looked like a child who has unexpectedly won a prize on speech day.

"Yes, indeed. Through my mother. My paternal

grandfather, as far as we know, was not entitled to bear arms. With the title, my father became automatically armigerous, of course. He chose the Clare arms as a compliment to my mother, though naturally our coat is different from the original grant. The chevrons are quartered with a variation on the city arms of Gloucester. The Red Hand of Ulster is included for the baronetcy and—"

Joe said, "Oh, God."

His father faltered, and his face lost the expression of enthusiasm that had briefly animated it.

"Fascinating," Dougal said. He tried glaring at Joe, who gratifyingly looked away. He nodded toward the arms above the fireplace. "That must be closer to the original grant. The earl's coronet as well."

"Ah, yes, the earldom of Gloucester, you know. In fact that coat is entirely anachronistic. A harmless, sentimental conceit. This castle once belonged to the Clares. I like to think we have our roots here."

Joe could no longer be contained. "That's moonshine, Pa. You know it is. There's no proof that Grandma's family had anything to do with them."

Sir Thomas straightened his shoulders. Dougal had the momentary illusion that he had expanded to fill his clothes. The baronet had been touched on his sorest point, which made him not only angry but loquacious.

His mother's great-grandfather had married a Cuthbertson of Devon. A Cuthbertson of Dorset had most certainly married a descendant of the Clares in 1526. A descendant on the distaff side, naturally. It was a moral certainty that the two Cuthbertsons were lineally connected. Severe deficiencies in the relevant parish records had unfortunately prevented Sir Thomas from attaining documentary proof.

"Two hundred years." He ran his fingers through his scanty hair. "A mere six generations. It's so frustrating. Even the, ah, genetic evidence supports the hypothesis. The Clares were known to be redheaded, on the whole. I used to have red hair. And look at Joe now."

Dougal did. He thought muddy carrot would have been a more accurate description. He smiled at Graver and tried to look suitably impressed by his host's arguments.

"May I see Zelda now?"

Sir Thomas cleared his throat. "It's very difficult, Mr.—"

"Of course you can't." Joe advanced, waving the rifle impartially between his father and his captive. He addressed his father. "He's bluffing. You know what Alex said."

"I know what Vertag said," Graver snapped. "Not that it necessarily has much bearing on what happened."

"He's a damn sight more reliable than Uncle James. You and Grandma trust that man far too much. He's a *crook*—can't you get that it into your head? And so's his friend *Mr.* Dougal over there. You don't like Alex because of his name and his nationality, but you go all gentlemanly with these two just because someone's told them not to say 'pleased to meet you' or 'toilet.' Dear *God.*"

"I won't have that sort of talk in my house, d'you

hear? Mr. Dougal, I apologize for this, ah, unseemly wrangling."

The dark flush of anger ebbed from Joe's face, leaving a sea of chalky white with freckled islands.

"Look, Father. What do we know about this guy? Uncle James implied he was some kind of a hit man. First he was meant to be working for us and then he's not. Now he turns up out of the blue and expects us to welcome him with open arms. The sensible thing to do is to lock him up until Alex gets back."

Dougal laughed as best he could. "I think James has been exaggerating my credentials. As I understand it, we're working together. I'm afraid we've all fallen victim to James's mania for not letting his left hand know what his right hand is doing."

"Very possibly." Sir Thomas stared at his feet. He looked like a weary and worried garden gnome.

In the awkward silence that followed, Dougal tried and failed to find some way to seize the initiative. It was plain that he was in a no man's land in a family battle of ideals: Thos looked back and Joe looked forward, but they were both dreamers, though with conflicting nightmares. Dougal and Zelda had somehow got caught in the crossfire.

But he was no nearer discovering what the battle was all about.

Joe destroyed the fragile family truce.

"I'm going to put him in the east wing." He gave a laugh that edged toward hysteria. "I hope you like rats, you smarmy bastard."

Graver lifted his head. "That will do, Joseph." The

117

words sounded like a formula that Sir Thomas had used with varying degrees of success for twenty-odd years. "We shall take him to our guest. There's no need to be uncivilized. I suggest we give your grandmother the casting vote."

Father and son stared at one another for a moment. Dougal shifted uneasily in his chair. For an instant he forgot why he was here and felt the familiar embarrassment of an outsider involved in a family quarrel.

"All right, Pa." Joe's eyes flickered toward Dougal. His voice retained its earlier venom. "We can leave the rats till later. Grandma *loves* making decisions."

They left the library in a procession: Graver was on Dougal's left, while Joe brought up the rear with the rifle. They turned right into the long, dusty passage that ran along the north side of the house toward the gatehouse.

Graver kept up a running commentary, like a host making conversation with an awkward guest. Or perhaps he merely wished to prevent Joe from saying anything.

He apologized for the condition of the building and mentioned death duties with a sorrowful solemnity that verged on pride. After all, death duties were a sort of hereditary disease, like gout; at least the sufferer could console himself with the thought that present discomfort was symptomatic of past luxuries.

Sir Thomas paused by one of the windows and peered down at the courtyard below. Much of it was occupied by a formal garden running wild in the summer.

"At least," he said quietly, as if to himself, "I've done some work on the house and ruins."

It sounded like a defense. Or even an epitaph.

Graver pointed out the stone facing on the northwest tower, which he had replaced in the spring. Joe shuffled in the background. Dougal peered over his host's shoulder, through the gaps in the curtain wall, and down into the forest, where Malcolm should be.

The river Wye shone yellow in the setting sun. The dense mass of trees gave nothing away.

"Shall we go on?" Sir Thomas asked politely. He ushered Dougal along the corridor. "We used to have the Reynolds there." He pointed at a rectangle of lighter paint on the wall. "And there was a lovely little Bellini horse in the alcove at the head of the stairs."

The stairwell was square, paneled in dark Tudor oak. They descended to the wide, stone-flagged hall and out into the open air. Immediately to their right was the gatehouse.

"Look," Joe said. "See those holes in the vault of the gateway? They were used for pouring boiling oil on unwanted visitors."

Dougal said nothing, allowing the remark to reverberate in the sudden silence.

Graver spoke, his voice heavy with embarrassment: "The herb garden." He waved his hand at the tangle of plants before them. "Not original, of course. My mother laid it out." He reached into a clump of gray-green spikes, then sniffed his fingers. "Rosemary. That's for remembrance, isn't it?"

He led the way along a graveled path through the garden toward the center of the west curtain wall. He trotted down a flight of steps with worn stone treads and pushed open a narrow door.

The glare of the dying sun shone straight into Dougal's eyes. Details emerged one by one. Beyond the postern was a broad terrace. Two deck chairs stood near the low wall at its edge. Zelda was on the left and an old woman on the right. There was a table between them, holding a tea tray and a gaily painted backgammon board. A game was in progress.

Zelda said, "William," and sucked in her breath. Dougal nearly laughed with the relief of finding her. But surely she could have escaped from such a geriatric guard.

"This is Mr. Dougal. My mother, Lady Graver."

Joe shuffled his feet behind them. Sir Thomas rubbed his nose, perhaps to check if it were still there.

Lady Graver slowly raised her hand; the fingers were laden with rings and twisted with arthritis.

"How do you do, Mr. Dougal. Welcome to Elmney."

Dougal gingerly shook her hand, wondering if he was expected to kiss it. Lady Graver had the *grande dame* manner, but it was probable that she would consider hand kissing to be an un-English habit, an unhygienic intimacy practiced south of Calais.

Lady Graver's left hand remained on her lap. It held a large, pearl-handled revolver.

"Mother, I must talk to you." Graver's voice had a quaver in it that shattered the stillness of the tableau.

"Hullo, love." Dougal stepped forward and kissed

120

Zelda decorously on the cheek. Her eyes, brown and moist, stared at him, full of questions he couldn't answer.

"One minute, dear." Lady Graver reproved both her son and Dougal. "This won't take long. It's my go and I'll double you. That will bring us up to eight pounds."

"No way." Zelda's voice was rich and firm. Dougal suddenly realized that she was a lot more than a maiden in distress: she was a potential ally.

"In that case, we leave it at four." Lady Graver opened a memorandum pad, cased in black leather, and extracted a silver pencil from its spine. "That will bring it up to twenty-seven pounds, fifty pence. Perhaps your luck will change this evening." Her tone abruptly sharpened. "Joseph, you should be in the kitchen. The vegetables."

Lady Graver swiftly made her dispositions. Dougal and Zelda were sent to the far end of the terrace and ordered to admire the view. Sir Thomas took Zelda's deck chair.

Dougal entertained a wild hope of leaping from the terrace hand in hand with Zelda. He was swiftly disabused. The terrace was a natural platform of rock nearly twenty feet above the ground. Even if they survived the landing without broken limbs, Graver with his .22 and Lady Graver with her revolver would make short work of them.

The Gravers' conversation—tetchily staccato on the one hand and thinly apologetic on the other—was undistinguishable. Dougal found Zelda's hand; their fingers slid together as if nature had designed them to be compatible.

"Aw, honey. Thank God you're here."

Zelda was wearing tight jeans and a green silk shirt; she looked as alluring as a dark-skinned Restoration beauty. A sharp twinge of desire, wholly inappropriate to the time and place, made Dougal tremble. He squeezed her hand—even that was exciting—and said:

"How have you been treated? What's happened?"

Her eyes slid away from the forest and looked at him. "Well, you could say that life's been a touch unsettling. I woke up yesterday with a gun in my ear, with a guy I'd never seen before at the other end of it. What the hell you got yourself into, William? Why didn't you level with me the other night?"

"I wanted to tell you. I just didn't want to drag you into it." He tried to gather his thoughts: speed, succinctness, and conviction were all essential. "I met Hanbury earlier this year and he got me . . . entangled in his activities for a few days. He's the bloke who snatched you, you know? It finished with me never wanting to see him again. Then last week he offered me a lot of money to get friendly with Joe Graver and an American called Vertag. Have you seen him here?"

Zelda shook her head. "They talk about him a lot, though, and he's meant to be visiting with them this evening. Joe likes him, but the other two don't."

"Joe and Alex Vertag are both members of organizations that are preparing for the holocaust. The end of the world. Hanbury said he had business interests with Vertag and wanted an eye kept on him, while he was in England."

"Why did you do it?"

"Hanbury backed up the offer with a little moral persuasion. I didn't know he was bluffing until yesterday. But in any case I'd decided to quit the night I met you. I heard that Vertag killed someone."

"Bert?" Zelda met Dougal's look of astonishment with a smile. "Sweetheart, these people treat me like one of the family. The only difference is, I don't get to carry a gun. None of them can stop talking—they're all running scared of something and they agonize about it all the time. All except the old woman, who cheats at backgammon and treats the men like they were halfway through first grade. Vertag killed this guy Bert—he was an informer, right?—and now Joe and his dad have to get rid of the body. They don't like that at all. It kind of confuses them too—because they thought someone else was going to do all the dirty work."

"What do you mean?"

"The Gravers think you're a killer. Hanbury's hired hand. You got quite a reputation around here."

"Zelda, I *swear* I'm not a bloody assassin. I don't know what's going on around here. Maybe they're trying to set me up for something. And you. I just want to get you out."

"I just love the way you say *bloody,*" Zelda said inconsequentially.

"So British. I never thought you were a killer. I trust my intuition. Anyway, they're treating you and me as if we belong to the same category of houseguest."

123

"Can you tell me what happened? Quickly?"

"Hanbury brought me here, in the back of a car. He stuck a needle in me in London that knocked me out for the trip—I don't even know where we are."

"The Forest of Dean. Just inside the Welsh border."

"He delivered me like a mailman with a parcel and vanished. Which doesn't please Lady Graver and old Tom. They locked me up in an old nursery in the part of the house they don't use. It's got bars on the windows and rocking horses on the wallpaper. Weird. They let me out for meals and to play backgammon. The murder screwed them all up; they're worried about money; and they made a lot of fuss about having what they called 'the last shipment' in the cellars. I think it went this afternoon and they were feeling quite cheerful. Until you turned up. But I wouldn't say they've ever been one big happy family—a lot of infighting goes on all the time about who gets to do the dishes and whose turn it is to empty the garbage."

"No staff inside the building?"

"Uh-huh. I think maybe a couple of women come in once or twice a week to clean. I've never seen anyone except the family. But there must be a few farmhands or gardeners."

They had been talking softly in near whispers, but Dougal lowered his voice still further:

"Malcolm's somewhere in the forest. We've got a van parked a mile or so away. We—"

"William Dougal!" Lady Graver's high-pitched voice hailed him as if they were separated not by four yards but by a quarter of a mile of stormy ocean.

Dougal reluctantly let go of Zelda's hand and swung

round. Lady Graver's gun hand beckoned him forward. Her son was struggling to escape from his deck chair.

"*Please* don't excite her," Graver whispered as he passed Dougal. "She's very old."

Lady Graver pointed him to the vacant deck chair. She stared at him for a moment, absently waving her revolver like a veteran conductor leading a sprightly but undemanding allegro.

At last the unnerving movement stopped; the stillness was worse, for the gun barrel was in line with Dougal's chest.

Adagio.

"Play backgammon, do you?"

"Yes." Dougal remembered with nostalgic clarity those ouzo-sodden evenings in the tavernas of Lindos. The triumphant click of the counters as gray-haired Greeks moved them at twice the speed of sound.

"Good. We'll play after dinner, if we have the opportunity."

Her sunken cheeks dug deeper into her skull. Her rouge glowed like fever spots, and the band of lipstick in the vicinity of her lips grew wider, like an expanding pool of blood. It might have been a rictus of hate, but Dougal was inclined to take it as a smile.

"You fond of that gel?"

Dougal nodded.

Her leer was as unexpected as a grin on the face of a tiger. "Enjoy it while you can, that's what I've always said."

"I try." Dougal's mouth was dry.

"James was right about you. He said you did unexpected things. And you handled my son very well.

Left to himself, he would have believed anything you told him."

"But you don't?"

"Of course not. James has kept me fully up-to-date about your position. We find it better to present a simpler version to my son."

Lady Graver paused. Her eyes swung away from Dougal and settled on the forest.

"His head is stuffed with romantic twaddle. My son's a fool, Mr. Dougal, like his father before him. Though at least his father had the knack of making money. But you're not a fool, and I want to know why you've come here."

Dougal counted ten before answering.

"I came to fetch Zelda. It's purely personal—I no longer have any other interests with James or with you. I'm not a threat to you in any way. Tell me," he added, as blandly as he was able, "how do you come to be mixed up with a pair of crooks like Vertag and James?"

"James is *not* a crook. He is my godson. I've known him all his life." Her tone was so vehement that the sentences almost seemed to be logically connected. "Since my husband died, he has acted as my financial adviser."

"So he set up a connection between you and Vertag? A sort of transatlantic mutual benevolence society?"

Lady Graver laughed. "But of course. Have you any notion what it costs to run a place like this? It doesn't seem to matter who's ruling the country; costs keep rising and one has to make ends meet. You know your Mr. Micawber."

126

"Only too well," Dougal agreed. She seemed, he thought, to be mellowing, though none of the credit was his. "But your fund-raising activities are no concern of mine—or Zelda's. Someone—Vertag perhaps?—has made a grotesque mistake—"

"If you won't tell me why you've come, perhaps you'll tell me how." Lady Graver switched her attack to another ill-defended position. "Hey?"

"I came by train," Dougal improvised. "To Gloucester. The taxi dropped me at the lodge gates, because I felt like a walk."

It sounded thin to him. Lady Graver looked as if she could see straight through it and out the other side. She might be mad; she was certainly uninhibited; but she wasn't a fool.

"*Bal*derdash." Lady Graver yawned, revealing a perfectly white set of dentures. "Not that it matters. Now you're here, you have a part to play. Both of you. James and I have discussed it several times."

"What do you want us to do?"

"Do? You won't have to *do* anything. You can leave all that to us. Just grin and bear it, eh?"

Dougal moved involuntarily. The chair creaked as his weight shifted.

Lady Graver laughed. "It's impossible to do anything dramatic in a deck chair," she observed. "And perhaps I should tell you that my Colt has a hair trigger. You were looking at my hands: arthritis is a sore trial, but as yet it hasn't had an appreciable effect on my reflexes."

Graver hurried to his mother and tenderly helped her to her feet. He found her walking stick beside her chair; it looked more like a weapon than a crutch.

"We will walk behind our young friends. If they become restive, you will shoot. So shall I. Go for the legs. I believe the backs of the knees are particularly vulnerable."

CHAPTER 12

The shadows now covered most of the courtyard. The remaining splashes of light glowed on the stonework, emphasizing without brightening the enclosure.

Dougal and Zelda were side-by-side. Their pace, dictated by Lady Graver's age and infirmities, gave the occasion an odd stateliness. Dougal was reminded of a wedding procession—possibly in the Wild West, since both the best man and the matron of honor were armed.

Lady Graver's hoarse directions reached them every few seconds: "slower . . . we turn right here . . . wait in that doorway on the left of the gatehouse . . . in you go . . . Thomas, for heaven's sake look where you're going."

They were in the east wing of the house now. It had been added in the nineteenth century and looked as if no one had had much to do with it since the death of Queen Victoria. The wallpaper was peeling and splotched with damp. The first flight of stairs was guarded by a line of stags' heads. Cobwebs linked the antlers. One head had lost its eyes.

Their speed decreased as they climbed. Lady Graver made no complaint, but her breath rasped behind them.

After the first floor, the stairs narrowed and their shoes clattered on the bare boards. The rubber tip of Lady Graver's stick clumped behind them. The musty scent of dry rot was everywhere. Dougal hoped they had deathwatch beetle as well.

The climb ended on the second floor. Dougal and Zelda were herded along a passage, with six closed doors on their right and two small windows, overlooking the courtyard, on their left.

The passage ended with a wall of unplastered stone, in the center of which was a low doorway surmounted by an ogee arch. Even in this weather, the crumbling mortar glistened with damp. The door was made of oak and bound with iron: heavyweight Victorian Gothic. There were two bolts.

Lady Graver told Dougal to open the door. The bolts protested and left smears of rust on his hands. He pulled the door open and cool air rushed out to meet him. His initial impression of the room beyond was of a dark hole, shot with slivers of light.

The tip of the walking stick rammed into the small of his back and propelled him over the threshold. Dougal missed the step down and stumbled into the room. Lady Graver clearly understood the psychological value of making your opponent feel foolish.

The darkness receded as Dougal's eyes adjusted to the gloom. They were in a round chamber, which must be the top story of the southeast tower. Three arrow slits, deep within their embrasures, and the open door provided the only light. There were rafters high above them and the suggestion of a stooped roof. A fireplace with a mutilated stone canopy stood on their left.

Something—half heard and half seen—scratched or slithered by the far wall.

"Rats," said Lady Graver with great satisfaction.

"*Rats.* Dougal shivered. He had met rats, dead and alive, in Acton and Katmandu, in Fez and Istanbul. Regardless of nationality, they inspired sheer terror.

"That's nice, we'll have company." It was his own voice, speaking from a million miles away.

"Lie down on your fronts."

The rough-grained wood of the floorboards was caked with decades of dust and bird droppings. Dougal stretched out a questing hand and met Zelda's on the same errand. The walking stick crunched against his knuckles.

"Hands by your sides, please. Thomas, untie his bootlaces."

Graver fumbled with Dougal's laces. His mother's footsteps, punctuated by the tap of the stick, shuffled between her two prisoners. Dougal raised his head. She was staring down at him with the revolver trained at his head.

"I used to come up here to shoot rats, young man. With this same gun. My husband thought it was un-ladylike."

"I daresay the rats did, too," said Dougal.

Sir Thomas at length mastered the principle of untying double granny knots. Dougal wondered if his hostess suspected him of suicidal tendencies.

But Lady Graver had other ideas: one shoelace was for Dougal's thumbs and the other for Zelda's. Graver, breathing heavily, knotted it so tightly that Dougal grunted with pain.

Her next instruction took both her son and her captives by surprise. She ordered Graver to bend back Dougal's leg and slip his foot behind the loop of his bound thumbs. Dougal's spine arched under the strain. His arms tried painfully and vainly to leave their sockets.

"Now the girl, Thomas." Lady Graver playfully tapped Dougal on the head with her walking stick. "Clever, isn't it? So economical. It quite took my fancy when James mentioned it. He learned how to do it in the Commandos."

Dougal, his head rearing back from his shoulders like the figurehead on a ship, said that he found it difficult to visualize James as a Commando; in any case, were these precautions really necessary?

"You could see it as a compliment. Zelda by herself was no problem. We just locked you up occasionally, didn't we, dear? But you are different. James quite admires you; he says you're lucky. I always make it a rule in games of chance to avoid unnecessary risks. Particularly with lucky people."

"Why not play dangerously for a change?" Dougal had to keep talking. It was much more dignified than whimpering.

"It won't be for long. Until James comes back. If circumstances permit, I should like to have a little backgammon tournament after dinner."

"Mother, perhaps—"

Lady Graver stopped her son with a look so virulent that he stepped backward. Zelda's body bucked like a

132

landed fish. Her teeth sunk into Graver's calf, just above the ankle. He shrieked—the pitch was unexpectedly high—and instinctively lashed out at Zelda with his other foot. The kick caught her on the side of her head and glanced down to her shoulder. She cried out.

Dougal snarled.

Zelda dropped six words into the ensuing silence: "I sure hope it goes septic."

"Stop whining, Thomas, and come along."

The heavy door slammed. Metal squealed as the bolts were thrust home. The only sound came from within the room itself: the ragged breathing of Dougal and Zelda.

"William. I think rats are kind of scary."

"Me too. Can't stand them. At least Graver was limping as he went out. It must have been a good bite. Your head okay?"

"Could be worse. But we'll get cramps soon and then I won't notice a sore head. You do yoga?"

"No."

"Neither do I. I've a feeling we're going to regret it."

"We could try shouting."

It was a feeble suggestion, for there was no one to hear, even if their cries reached the outside world.

Zelda didn't bother to answer. Dougal thought of Zelda's sharp white teeth.

"Could we move closer together? My laces are pretty frayed. It might be possible to gnaw through them."

Besides, if they moved, it might persuade the rats to keep their distance. He forced away the shockingly vivid image of long-tailed, dark brown rodents scurry-

133

ing over their trussed bodies. Gleaming eyes and sharp teeth.

He turned his head, wincing at the extra strain on the contorted muscles of his neck. Zelda was two or three yards away, but it might as well have been the distance between New York and London. His right thigh began to throb, adding a basso profundo to the already impressive orchestral range of his pain.

An interval followed in which time lay outside the jurisdiction of clocks and calendars. Even gravity seemed suspended for the occasion; it was as if the floor was impelled from beneath to push its malignant surface against Dougal's thinly covered body.

Zelda was the first to move. Using her left, unbound leg as a lever, she rolled onto her side. Dougal copied her action. They inched together. Neither spoke; any surplus breath was required for grunting.

Dougal had his back to Zelda. He wondered if it was easier to go forward than backward in this unnatural position. Each time his body writhed, the distance covered seemed to be shorter. It was possible that he wasn't moving at all.

He felt some portion of her anatomy touch his leg. *Not a rat, please God.* His hopes leaped, but it took another eternity before he felt her warm breath on his hands.

His eyes closed. In the darkness Zelda's teeth nipped impartially at the shoelace and his thumbs. His hands grew wet. Sweat or spit? He didn't care. The pains arching through his body reached a savage, sustained harmony, which was pushing his thoughts out of control. Sensation was transposed to sound: the music pierced him. The darkness behind his eyes was split by fractured lines of light. The pain wreathed its way through his muscular system like a nest of white vipers on the march.

Mustn't faint. Mustn't scream.

Amo, amas, amat, amamus, amatis, amant, amabam, amabas, amabat, amabamus, amabatis, amabant, amem—no, that's subjunctive—amabo, amabis, ama—

The last strands of the lace parted.

Dougal shuddered as his limbs jerked back to more comfortable positions. He hauled himself on to his knees. As he swayed there, his hands swung up to his mouth of their own accord. They were covered with blood; it tasted nourishing.

He crawled behind Zelda and found her knotted hands. He held them apart and chewed in his turn. The action triggered a wholly unexpected memory: the clasping of hands at a degree ceremony, the descendant of a medieval act of fealty.

Zelda's body heaved. Her liberated leg flailed forward, catching Dougal's shoulder and sending him sprawling on his back.

They lay in silence and watched the pain ebbing.

"Won't Malcolm go to the police?"

Dougal looked up from threading the remains of the laces into his boots; he really would have to buy some new ones. "Not Malcolm. He knows he's got nothing to convince a policeman. Besides, Graver's a JP; he's the neighborhood grandee. No local copper would bust in here without a warrant. And for another thing, Malcolm tends to avoid the police, not seek them out."

"So he'll either come looking for you himself or decide to cut his losses, right?" Zelda sounded perfectly calm, as if they were engaged in nothing more exciting than a game of backgammon.

"Right." Dougal stared round their dimly lit, cylindrical prison. He remembered bitterly that reliability was not one of Malcolm's virtues; at this very moment he could be dallying with a comely ploughboy in a village pub. He tried to look on the bright side: "If Malcolm comes, at least he's got a gun."

"You got strange friends," Zelda said slowly. "So have the Gravers. If we don't get out somehow, they're going to kill us. I can feel it."

Dougal tried to say something reassuring, but Zelda shook her head.

"Sweetheart, they wouldn't have talked so openly to us if they planned to let us go. No way."

"Damn it." Dougal's voice was quiet, but he was shivering with anger. "And we don't even know *why.*"

Zelda halfheartedly brushed some of the dirt from her jeans. "Yeah, seems unfair. Kind of adds insult to injury. God, I wish I could wash my hair. And I haven't brushed my teeth since Friday morning."

"We'll go over the room," Dougal said obstinately. "Walls, ceilings, floor. There might be another way out. If they come back or when they come back, we'll jump them. They'll expect us to be tied up. Go for the crotch, I suppose."

"I've got long, strong fingernails." Zelda displayed them. Her red nail varnish was chipped. "I'm going for the eyes. We had a rape class, last semester. Pity we haven't got a set of keys. You could put them through your fingers."

"Oh, God," Dougal said.

"I know, honey."

They were silent for a moment. Violence was like death: you took it for granted that the universe had granted you a personal exemption from an otherwise omnipresent phenomenon. On balance, Dougal decided, he was more afraid of violence than of dying. At least no one brought back traveler's tales of death.

"Why did I bother to give up smoking?" Dougal thought of despair as a football and kicked it off his mental pitch. "Come on. Let's look over the room while there's still some light left."

The floorboards were still sound; the oak planks lay firm and flush beside each other, a tribute to the craft of some long-dead carpenter. The rafters were too high to reach, even if Dougal stood on Zelda's shoulders. They verified this empirically.

The chimney's narrowness belied the breadth of the fireplace's canopy. The arrow slits were too small to squeeze through and too high to jump from. Zelda stared out of the one that overlooked the gatehouse and part of the drive, while Dougal gave the door its second examination in five minutes.

"Hey!" Zelda said. Her foot smashed through the lower half of the window pane. "Hey! Help!" She was shouting now, crouching to bring her head to the level of the hole. Her voice mingled with the tinkle of falling glass.

Dougal rushed into the embrasure and peered over

Zelda's head. Then he was shouting as well.

Outside in the twilight, a uniformed figure was walking briskly up the drive. At this distance, and in this light, it was difficult to be sure. But it looked as if the figure was wearing a dark blue uniform and a flat cap. Even as they watched, the figure gave what might have been a wave in their direction, before vanishing over the edge of their field of vision.

"God!" Zelda's voice was hoarse, somewhere between a prayer and a question. "Don't tell me that isn't a cop."

CHAPTER 13

"Officer," said Lady Graver, pronouncing the first syllable *orf;* the other two syllables emerged in an outraged hiss. "I take it you are aware who I am? That your chief constable reports to my son?"

"Yes, my lady."

The constable's obsequiousness goaded her further.

"You have entered a private dwelling without permission from the owner and without a warrant. You have used violence toward a lady, without any provocation. You bruised my arm severely, you know. I shall have it seen by a doctor. You are forcing your attention on two of my guests. By God, officer, you won't be an officer by the time I've finished with you."

The constable nodded encouragingly. "Early retirement has always attracted me."

"When policemen stopped wearing helmets and started riding around in those silly cars: that's when the rot set in. You're no better than the bloody Gestapo, d'you hear?"

"If you won't give me your stick, I'll just have to take it."

Lady Graver swung the stick back, her mouth tightening with determination. The slow, tired movement of her arm mocked the hatred in her eyes. Dougal and Zelda grabbed her, one at each side. Her arms felt as frail as a famine victim's.

Malcolm tipped his cap back at an insouciant angle and smiled. Dougal passed the stick to him. Lady Graver fell back to the center of the room, her hands clutching the strap of her handbag.

"Drop your bag, Ma."

Dougal glanced curiously at him. Malcolm was enjoying himself, no doubt about it. He held Lady Graver's pearl-handled Colt in one hand and her stick in the other. The walking stick marred the swashbuckling effect; by rights it should have been a saber.

Lady Graver raised her eyes and said, with a queer dignity, "No, young man. My handbag is private."

It was as if Malcolm had threatened to break one of the great moral laws of the universe: that a lady's handbag should be sacrosanct. The bag was unlikely to contain anything that Malcolm needed—just the material symbols of Lady Graver's personality.

"Malcolm," Dougal began, realizing simultaneously that not only was he too late, but he shouldn't have mentioned their rescuer's name.

Malcolm stepped forward, the stick under his arm, and separated her fingers from the strap. "Mustn't take any chances, must we?"

"You despicable little rat." Lady Graver spat at his

face, but couldn't reach it. A dribble of spittle ran unnoticed down her chin.

Malcolm laughed.

Dougal turned sharply and left the room. The others followed. Malcolm shot home the bolts. Dougal could hear Lady Graver beginning to cry: old, dry sobs, rusty with disuse.

"That was unnecessary," he said quietly.

Malcolm shrugged. "Maybe. Better to be sure with a woman like that." He riffled through the handbag, taking a bunch of keys and the cash from the purse. He propped the stick against the wall and left the ravished handbag on the nearest windowsill.

Zelda broke the silence as they walked along the landing: "Am I glad to see you. How did you do it?"

"When William didn't turn up at our rendezvous, I carried on round the castle, hoping to meet him en route. And there you all were on the terrace. After you all went in, I nipped back to the van. You like the uniform? I think it's rather fetching. Dark blue suits me."

"You got it from the same bloke as you got the van? The theatrical costumier?" Dougal asked.

"That's right. It was in that box in the back. I borrowed it on impulse." Malcolm paused at the head of the stairs and grinned back at them. "Pity I couldn't get a patrol car to match. I had to walk up the drive. Then I simply rang the doorbell. Lady Graver answered. After I had twisted her arm a little, she brought me up to you."

"Thank you," said Dougal formally. He wondered

whether to interpret the arm twisting literally or metaphorically. His mind ran on: if they could avoid Graver and Joe, if they could leave before Hanbury or Vertag turned up . . . "Let's go. We could go over the north wall and round through the forest."

"No, not yet. If we run now, the whole business could blow up again. We're on a winning streak now. It would be far better to follow it for a while."

"What do you mean?" Zelda stared at Malcolm with open-eyed amazement, as if she was seeing him properly for the first time. Malcolm often had the effect of appearing big, bright, and unpredictable to women. The fact that he was so patently uninterested in them only served to increase the fascination he exercised; Malcolm modestly ascribed the phenomenon to his charisma.

He smiled at her. "We have a chance to find out what's happening. It'd be stupid to let it slide. Who's at home just now?"

"Joe and his dad. Vertag and Hanbury are expected, but no one seems to know when. That's all."

"Well, there you are." Malcolm waved the Colt in an expansive manner that was oddly reminiscent of Lady Graver. "It's a golden opportunity to immobilize the Gravers as well. Minimize the possibility of pursuit. They'll soon start looking for the old hag upstairs if we leave them to their own devices."

"Are they your only reasons?" Dougal was alerted by a hint of smug anticipation in Malcolm's tone.

"We have to make a living. These people have put us to an awful lot of trouble and expense. I don't see why we should walk away empty-handed unless we have to."

"You wanna *burglarize* them?"

"Zelda, *please.*" Malcolm managed to imply that years of intimacy lay behind them. "Conventional morality is relative to conventional life. Circumstances alter cases. Take wars, for example. This is a private war and it's got its own rules. *We* didn't choose to wage it. Hanbury cheated William out of a lot of money. He shanghaied you. God knows what the Gravers were going to do to you both. Vertag's a killer, and his methods of implementing his apocalyptic *Reich* make Eichmann's seem positively philanthropic. They've all put themselves beyond the law, and we have to deal with them as such. If we turn the other cheek, they'll go right ahead and slap it."

"I guess you're entitled to your point of view." Zelda pushed her hair away from her eyes and said crisply, "In any case, I got to find my bags. And my passport. How would we handle the Gravers?"

"A short, sharp shock?" said Malcolm vaguely. "We can play it by ear."

"No." The others looked at Dougal as if he were an adult announcing bedtime to a couple of excited children. "You're being absurdly overconfident. They're armed. Hanbury or Vertag could turn up at any time."

"I tell you what," said Malcolm disarmingly, "if you agree to stay, you can be boss. You can make the ground rules. I'm staying, whatever. And I've got the keys to the van."

Dougal capitulated and accepted the guiding role that had been thrust upon him. It was the only way he could hope to contain Malcolm's reckless lust for booty within reasonable limits. Zelda's enthusiasm was harder to explain but equally in need of restraint. It was an unwelcome reminder of the extent to which their relationship was based on mutual ignorance. The twin sensations of priggishness and responsibility for the safety of others smothered him.

The practicalities were easier to deal with. Just as he had visualized the approaches to the castle in military terms earlier in the day, he found it a surprisingly simple matter to interpret their present situation as an exercise in tactics. As they moved down the stairs, he whispered his dispositions.

Zelda was to stay in the gatehouse tunnel, watching for any movement in the drive—or for that matter in the courtyard itself; Dougal and Malcolm would look for Thos, Joe and Zelda's belongings.

Malcolm fumbled in his tunic and produced the Webley, which had been making an unsightly bulge just above his midriff. He gave it to Dougal, retaining the Colt for himself. Dougal checked that the safety catch was on. The gun felt heavy and obtrusive in his hand, like a cumbersome talisman that belonged to someone else.

They slipped into the shadow-filled gate tunnel. The great gates were barred, but the postern cut into one leaf was ajar. Zelda stationed herself beside it, ready to close and bolt it if anyone approached. Having done that, she would ring the front doorbell to warn the others.

Dougal and Malcolm moved round to the front door. It was closed but unlocked. Dougal pushed it gently open, wincing as it creaked, and peered into the hall. Apart from the stairs, there were three doors: one led toward the bulk of the house; the second to the adjacent gate tower at ground level; and the third proved to lead to a cramped cloakroom built into the thickness of the curtain wall.

"You want to play policeman again? We might as well ring the doorbell. No point in looking for them when they will come to us."

Malcolm nodded. "And you?"

Dougal jerked his head toward the cloakroom. "I'll lurk behind the door. If both of them come down, an element of surprise could be useful. Tell Zelda what we're going to do before you ring the bell."

When ajar, the cloakroom door not only concealed Dougal but offered him a view of the stairs and of the door to the rest of the house, through the crack between it and the door frame.

The butt of the Webley grew warm in his hand. His breathing, he was pleased to note, was normal; his head was clear; he was not so much nervous as resigned to the inevitable. He wished Malcolm would hurry up.

The serrated ring of an electric bell cut through the silent hall. Dougal's ear strained after the sound as it tailed away into the vast house around them.

A door slammed. There were footsteps, which must mean that the movement emanated from upstairs; otherwise the sound would have been muffled by the door. Only one person was answering the bell.

Sir Thomas came into view at the bend on the stairs. His hands darted around his head, trying to smooth his wispy hair. He was wearing a kitchen apron, which carried the words TOO MANY COOKS SPOIL THE BROTH.

He hurried across the hall and opened the door.

"Sir Thomas Graver, sir?" Malcolm asked.

"Yes. What is it?" Graver's voice was sharp, the tone of a man who was used to dealing with policemen. The hesitation he showed when confronting members of his family and suspected criminals had vanished.

"We had a telephone call, sir. The inspector thought I'd better come round in person. In the circumstances. May I come in?"

"If you must," said Sir Thomas tetchily. "But I can only spare you a moment. What's all this about a telephone call?"

"An anonymous informant, sir. Gloucestershire's answer to Deep Throat, I daresay. I hardly like to pass on what he said."

"Come *on*, man."

"Our caller claimed that you had kidnapped two people and were holding them against their will here at the castle. Rubbish, of course. But we thought you might be able to give us an idea as to the identity of the caller. A disgruntled ex-employee, perhaps? Can you think of anyone who might bear a grudge against you?"

"Me." Dougal slid round the cloakroom door and had the barrel of the Webley against Graver's back before the man could turn. "Put your hands on your head."

146

"Officer," the baronet quavered, "this man is armed. I have reason to believe—"

His words were blocked by a sound that was close to a sob. He had seen the gun that had appeared in Malcolm's hand—and recognized it as his mother's.

Malcolm patted Graver's pockets, finding nothing besides a tobacco pouch and a set of car keys. He produced a set of handcuffs from his own pocket and shackled the baronet's wrists behind his back. As he worked, Malcolm whistled under his breath. Dougal recognized the tune with a shock: Gilbert and Sullivan. The policeman's lot might not in general be a happy one, but Malcolm was certainly enjoying his spot of constabulary duty.

"My mother . . . " Graver whispered.

Dougal felt as if he had been kicked in the stomach. "She's okay." He intended his tone to be brutal, but it came out reassuring. "She'll stay that way if you do as you're told. Where's Joe?"

"In the kitchen. We were cooking dinner. Is my mother hurt? Where is she?"

Malcolm prodded the Colt into Graver's midriff. "Anyone else in the house? What about Vertag and Hanbury?

"Vertag's meant to be coming this evening, I don't know when. I don't know where Hanbury is, I swear it."

Malcolm suddenly flung his left arm round Graver's neck, squeezed it, and forced the man to his knees. He scratched the tip of Graver's nose with the sight that protruded from the end of the Colt's barrel. "Sure, my little man?"

147

"That's enough," Dougal snapped. "Let him stand up."

Graver's eyes were like a spaniel's: brown sorrow.

"Lady Graver's comfort," Dougal continued, "is entirely dependent on your behavior. Take us to Joe and don't try to warn him."

"He'd be very silly to do that," Malcolm said, "because he'd be between us and Joe. In a no man's land, in fact."

Graver drew himself up to his full height and stared up at Dougal. "You disappoint me," he said. "I took you for a gentleman."

"No," Dougal said gently. "I'm afraid I'm not."

The kitchen came as a surprise. It was on the first floor, on the same level as the library, and had not been a kitchen for very long. Dougal had been expecting an immense undercroft with cavernous fireplaces and blackened ranges, not this small, bright room with a split-level oven. Orange wall units warred with the primrose yellow walls. The work surfaces were lined with sparkling labor-saving devices.

Joe was crouching in front of the lower door of a gigantic fridge-freezer. Frozen air billowed sluggishly around his body like tendrils of mist.

"Who was it?" he said without turning his head. "Are you sure there's some pita bread in here?"

"It's already warming in the oven," said Graver mechanically.

Malcolm was already bounding across the room. He seized Joe by the scruff of his neck and flung him face downward. Joe's glasses clattered on the floor.

Joe squawked as Malcolm dropped on top of him. The squawk became a yell as Malcolm bent his victim's left arm in a direction that nature had never intended it to take.

"Where's your gun?"

"On the table. *Please* let go."

"Shut up, punk."

Dougal, still covering Graver, crossed to the table underneath the window. He wished that Malcolm didn't have to be quite so violent.

The .22 lay between a pile of potato peelings and a dish of coleslaw. As he picked it up, he heard two raps, each followed by a tinkle.

Malcolm was using the butt of the pistol on the lenses of Joe's glasses. It was an act that belonged to the traditional repertoire of the playground bully. Dougal felt that he had become an active participant in a sadistic regression to childhood; God knew what Joe was feeling.

And yet: it was undoubtedly sensible to ensure that Joe was partially blind. The safety of Dougal, Malcolm, and Zelda might depend on it.

And yet.

"Search him," ordered Dougal hoarsely. Malcolm was already frisking his captive, combining business with pleasure in a comprehensive range of exploratory caresses.

Dougal turned back to Sir Thomas, who was watching events on the floor. "I want some twine; heavy string would do."

Graver hastily rearranged his features. "In the cupboard under the left hand sink . . . there's a Silver

Jubilee tin . . . shall I get it, Mr. Dougal?"

"Don't bother."

Dougal found the ball of string, cut off a length with the vegetable knife, and passed it to Malcolm.

"What about keys?" Malcolm asked. His hand was investigating Joe's left armpit.

"Behind the door." Graver darted toward it in an attempt to show his willingness to please. Then, realizing his action might be misinterpreted, he cast piteous looks at Dougal, which increased his resemblance to a spaniel still further.

"You stay there." It was less of an order than a reassurance.

There were two rows of keys, most of which were neatly labeled in faded black copperplate. The four exceptions were at the righthand end of the bottom row. Their labels were scrawled in red biro. Two of the hooks held sets of car keys; the numbers on the labels showed that both vehicles were last year's models; Dougal pocketed these. He left the third, WINE CELLAR, where it was, but hesitated over the fourth, GATEHOUSE UNDERCROFT. The hook held two keys, both of which looked freshly cut. Why should the Gravers have bothered to install both a Yale lock and a Chubb on the same door?

Covering the movement with his body, Dougal slipped the keys off the hook and into his pocket. He was about to swing the door back against the wall when he noticed a heavy, warded key on the row above: NURSERY.

"Is that where you kept Zelda?"

Graver stared at the floor and nodded.

150

"Good." Dougal thought about what they had done to Zelda, concentrating his anger until it became an effective ethical solvent; he had to strip away his scruples, if only temporarily.

"The nursery?" Malcolm said. He gave Joe's bottom a light slap. "Just the place for naughty children."

As Zelda said, there were rocking horses on the wallpaper and bars on the window. The room contained nothing else except an elderly camp bed and a pair of rumpled blankets.

Dougal pulled out the ball of string and cut off two more pieces. "Lash them to the windows, please. Joe first. Facing outward."

Malcolm's blunt fingers, deft through years of knot tying, swiftly obeyed. He spoke only to demand more string. The Gravers stood slackly, their eyes vacant. They might have been watching themselves on television.

You won't bite yourselves out of that one, thought Dougal in a halfhearted attempt to maintain the level of his anger. His eyes felt as if someone had rubbed them in red pepper.

He motioned Malcolm out onto the landing. They were on the top floor of the main house, which was as bare as the east wing.

"I'm going to question these two. Would you tell Zelda what happened? Give her the rifle and show her how to use it."

"Okay. Then I'll get a couple of bags and mooch around the house. You never know what you might find in an old barn like this."

Dougal pulled out the keys he had taken. "Check the vehicles first. We may need a car. Find out what they keep in the undercroft of the gatehouse. And have a look through Graver's papers in the library. They left my keys and penknife on the mantelpiece in there. Maybe you should look for Zelda's things after you've seen to the cars: two suitcases and a shoulder bag, I think—you'd better ask her."

"Don't worry." Malcolm patted Dougal's shoulder and moved along the landing. Raising his voice so that it was audible through the open door of the nursery, he called back, "I'd go for the hands, if I were you. The nerves there are *so* sensitive. I'll see if I can find an electric drill downstairs."

CHAPTER 14

"Please," said Joe, "get it over quickly, would you." His pallor accentuated his freckles. Fear sharpened his features, emphasizing their delicacy and explaining, in part at least, Malcolm's reprehensible behavior on the kitchen floor.

"My mother, Mr. Dougal . . . she's not in the best of health. I would be quite prepared—only too glad— I'm sure Joseph agrees with me—"

"Oh, shut up." Dougal patted his pockets without thinking. "I don't suppose either of you has a cigarette?"

"There's been no tobacco at Elmney since my father died." Sir Thomas shifted uneasily against the bars of the window. "I wish we could help."

Dougal turned away from those expectant, apologetic eyes. He tried to use up his surplus nervous energy by pacing up and down the room. One more turn of the screw would bring whatever information the Gravers had tumbling out. It would probably produce their life histories as well. All Dougal needed to do was to poke the barrel of the Webley into a tender portion of one of his captives. If physical torture was abhorrent, he could achieve much the same effect with a few imaginative predictions about the immediate future of Lady Graver.

But the screw wouldn't turn. Once again he had overestimated his capabilities, a mistake he was accustomed to make with alcohol rather than people. He wouldn't be able to torture this pathetic pair. He lacked the requisite moral fiber.

The silence in the nursery lengthened. It was almost a relief to hear footsteps in the corridor, for panic blotted out every other activity in Dougal's mind.

Malcolm eased his bulky torso round the door and hope died in the Gravers' eyes. He was wearing his Cheshire Cat grin. Dougal relaxed his grip on the Webley and tried to look as if he was leaning nonchalantly on the wall, not flattening himself against it.

"Evening, all." Malcolm grinned benevolently at the Gravers and returned the keys and penknife to Dougal. "These two dear people forgot to tell us about the safe. A natural oversight in the circumstances."

"Where is it?"

"Behind one of the bookcases in the library. The rest of the books on that wall are thick with dust. But not the collected sermons of the Venerable Archibald Lines in twelve calfbound volumes. It's a letter combination."

Both the Gravers looked mulishly vacant.

Malcolm's voice became menacing. "Come along, grandpa. Don't say it's 'Open Sesame' because we won't believe you."

His words were addressed to Sir Thomas, but his attention was on Joe. As he spoke, Malcolm ran the Colt over Joe's cheeks, first one then the other, like a monstrous electric razor.

Sir Thomas's tongue—surprisingly pink and pointed—emerged from his mouth and slowly moistened his thin, pale lips.

Malcolm forced the muzzle of the gun into Joe's mouth. Joe jerked his head as far back as it would go. His eyes rolled wildly downward, trying to focus on the Colt.

"Damn it," Dougal began, appalled both by Malcolm's actions and by the fascination they aroused in himself.

"All right," Sir Thomas said. "It's 'Cornucopia.' " He paused. "Shall I spell it?"

The tension that bound the four of them together in that hot, low-ceilinged room suddenly dissolved. Dougal fought the impulse to smile. Malcolm gently withdrew the barrel of the Colt and bellowed with laughter.

"If you're lying," he said as his chuckles subsided, "I'll blow a hole in Sonny Jim's left kneecap. Okay, grandpa?"

Without waiting for an answer, he turned round and faced Dougal. He groped in one of the capacious pockets of his tunic and produced a crumpled eight-by-six photograph. He held it out to Dougal.

"Found that in the library. It was in a frame lying face down in one of the desk drawers."

It was an enlarged snapshot, probably taken on the terrace of the castle. A much younger Lady Graver was grimacing at the camera. Her arm was draped casually across the shoulders of a good-looking boy in flannels and an open-necked shirt. There was a broad and instantly recognizable smile on his face.

James Hanbury.

"So that part of the story's true." Dougal glanced over his shoulder at the Gravers. "I wonder why they hid the photo."

"Ask them."

"Just a moment." Dougal beckoned Malcolm into the corridor. He closed and locked the door of the nursery, relieved to have escaped from those pitiful eyes. He looked down at the photograph and thought how improbable this youthful Hanbury seemed: like Athena, he had the appearance of having sprung full grown into life; it was difficult to imagine a time when Hanbury had not been a nattily tailored, dominant male in early middle age.

Malcolm pursed his lips. "He's put on a lot of weight since then, hasn't he? How are you getting on in there?"

"I'm not," said Dougal miserably. "They look so bloody pathetic. Old Thos cares more about his mother than he does about himself. Joe's as scared as I was an hour or so ago. And what's the point of interrogating them in any case? Hanbury and Vertag will have filled them up with lies."

"Chicken," said Malcolm without rancor.

Dougal held out his hand. "Let's have the keys for the undercroft. The sooner we've finished here the better."

"Okay." Malcolm dropped the two keys into Dou-

156

gal's palm and led the way to the head of the stairs. They separated on the next floor. Dougal continued down to the hall. He resisted the temptation to pop outside for a word with Zelda and tugged open the heavy door, which gave access to the ground floor of the nearer of the two gatehouse towers.

The room within was dimly lit by the original arrow slits. Dougal brushed his hand down the wall beside the door until he found the light switch. White-sheeted shapes sprang suddenly out of the darkness. Dougal lifted the corner of the nearest sheet and exposed an immense mahogany table leg, floridly carved and pockmarked with woodworm. A taller but slimmer ghost transpired to be a wardrobe with a cracked mirror and only three legs.

Everything was coated with a layer of dust with the exception of a scuffed track that ran from the door, hugging the wall, to a low archway in the corner.

The archway led onto a spiral staircase that snaked up—and down—through the thickness of the wall. The stone treads were worn, plunging into darkness. Dougal looked around for another light switch and immediately saw it at his shoulder. The white plastic casing of the switch was obviously new, as were the wires that ran from it.

He flicked the switch and ran down the stairs. The door at the bottom was new as well and looked as if it had been designed with battering rams in mind. It was a perfect match for the low stone archway that framed it. Its smooth surface was painted gray and felt metallic to the touch.

The keys from the kitchen turned quietly in the locks. Dougal pulled the door open and found another light switch.

His first impression was one of size. He had been expecting the undercroft to conform to the outline of the tower above it. Instead it stretched away far to his left, probably extending beneath the entire gatehouse. The roof—a double-barrel vault—was supported by a line of squat pillars constructed of the pink-tinged local stone. The pillars bisected the cellar, giving it the appearance of a rudimentary and lopsided chapel. The walls had recently been given a coat of whitewash. The air smelled fresh, cool, and dry. As far as he could see, the undercroft was empty.

In that case, why had it been redecorated, rewired, and given a brand new door with two locks?

Dougal moved round the room in a clockwise direction, staying close to the walls. Halfway toward the far end, he realized the room wasn't empty. Two of the dumpy pillars concealed what was evidently a loading bay. A section of the vault, perhaps six feet square, had been removed from the ceiling. A trapdoor filled the space, held there by two steel bars. A chute stretched from floor to ceiling. Beside it was an aluminum ladder. Three low, sturdy trolleys were propped up against the wall.

There was a smell in the air—an oddly familiar compound of oil and metal—which tugged at Dougal's memory. The smell obstinately refused to identify itself.

The position of the trapdoor was easier to work out.

158

If the undercroft matched the gatehouse above it, the chute must descend from the tunnel that connected the outside world with the courtyard. A pair of gates blocked the tunnel at either end—after all, this was a keep gatehouse, designed to continue its resistance when the rest of the castle had been overrun.

A picture grew in Dougal's mind: medieval amenities used for a modern purpose. A vehicle would drive into the gatehouse tunnel. Once both sets of gates were closed, it could be unloaded in complete privacy. Its contents would come down the chute and onto one of those trolleys. The tunnel was too small for a pantechnicon, but there would be plenty of room for one of the smaller Campernoyles vans.

He wondered if the smell of oil and metal was just one more sensory distortion caused by giving up smoking. For some reason it reminded him of going out after rabbits with his father. Dougal had been thirteen. His father's first shot had blown the head from an incautious young rabbit. Dougal had ruined this rare moment of masculine intimacy by being sick.

The click was as loud as an explosion in the silence of the undercroft.

It jerked Dougal out of the past and thrust him against the nearest pillar. His fingers probed the Webley, checking the safety catch was off. His attention darted out in the direction of the sound—toward the door. He felt, rather than heard, a faint displacement of air as the door opened. He edged round the pillar, both hands wrapped round the butt of the revolver. His gaze swept slowly along the wall toward the door, for a sudden movement could betray him. He caught a flash of blue at the edge of his field of vision.

Then the lights went out.

The door slammed. The sound unlocked Dougal from his trance and sent him edging back toward the wall. He had to have some guide to where he was. If only he had brought a torch.

He pushed the thought away, concentrating his mind on the tips of his fingers. He swept them to and fro as he moved, one step and a pause at a time. At last his hands brushed against the rough stone. He brought his other hand onto the wall. His left knee knocked into one of the trolleys that were propped against the wall.

Metal grated on stone. The trolley slid down the wall and crashed onto the stone flags.

Oh, God.

If anyone was with him in the undercroft, he now knew approximately where Dougal was. Dougal crouched down, his back against the wall, and listened.

The silence enveloped him, as impenetrably as the darkness. Dougal began to count, *One, two, three . . .* At first he planned to stop at five hundred. Fear made him extend his destination to a thousand.

By the seven hundreds, his eyes had begun to be useful again. Above his head he could just make out a faint rectangle, a lighter shade of darkness, which marked the outlines of the trapdoor. High on the far wall were two squares of light which perhaps showed the position of ventilation shafts up to the courtyard.

A thousand.

Whoever had turned off the lights had probably left. If the person was stalking Dougal, why the delay? Why turn the lights out?

He started to make a circuit of the walls, heading toward the door. He kept his left hand on the wall; the muscles of his right hand were aching quietly from the weight of the Webley. No one ever mentioned how heavy guns were. The butt of the revolver was clammy with sweat.

The worst part of the journey to the door was not the movement: it was the pauses in which Dougal had nothing to do but listen.

The plastic box of the light switch appeared under his fingers, just before he reached the door. Dougal allowed himself no time to think. He pushed the switch down and and leapt out from the wall. He ended in a crouch. Swiftly he turned through 360 degrees.

His mind had obligingly activated some deep-filed memory cell. Orders pumped out of the past: *right hand on pistol butt, left hand on wrist to steady it, point your gun upward so you can lower it for a snap shot, make yourself as small as possible to minimize the target you present.*

The undercroft was empty. For a second, Dougal unexpectedly felt cheated. He walked up and down its width to check that no one was lurking in the aisles. A small possibility remained that the intruder could have had time to take refuge behind a pillar.

He edged toward the door, patting his trousers to find which pocket held the keys. The Yale presented no problem: he had left the lock on the latch, where it still was. He inserted the key into the Chubb lock and turned gently in a counterclockwise direction. The lock refused to budge. Dougal increased the pressure, to no avail. He tried to turn the key clockwise: the tongue of the lock slid smoothly into the jamb of the door, coming to rest with a gentle, well-oiled click.

Dougal unlocked the door again and pulled out his penknife. He selected the larger of the two blades and ran it down between the jamb and the door. It met no obstacle: no bolts on the outside or concealed locks. For good measure he ran the blade round the rest of the door: there were no wedges driven into the top and bottom; and only the hinges interrupted the right-hand side.

The sound of his breathing seemed suddenly very loud. He glanced behind him, set his shoulder to the door, and pushed.

The door stayed blank, unmoving, and entirely hateful. Dougal's right foot, apparently acting at its own volition, lashed out at the base of the door.

The pain in his toes made him cry aloud. Dougal belatedly realized that a temper tantrum was not the best way to deal with a steel-reinforced door.

He leaned against the wall and tried to ignore the pain. The door must be wedged—easy enough to do in the confined space of the stairwell, with a wide range of potential props among the furniture in the room above.

Someone had taken the trouble to trap him, turning out the lights merely to complicate Dougal's life a little further. But no one had tried to kill him.

Yet.

His attention turned away from the web of speculation that threatened to engulf it. The ventilators were worth investigation.

Dougal walked down to the nearest one. He found a narrow opening, perhaps a foot square, cut into the curve of the vault. It was blocked by a grid of steel bars that looked as new as the wiring. The shaft above the grill curved away, presumably up to the courtyard. It made a dog's leg, which partly explained why it allowed so little light to filter down. The base of the tower, where the shaft must emerge, was obscured by a line of flowering shrubs.

"Zelda . . . *Zelda* . . . ZELDA!"

It was worth a try. If she was still in the gate passage, she might hear him, despite all the obstacles in the way. The *if* was a big one: whoever had confined Dougal was unlikely to have left Zelda and Malcolm at large.

There was no answer. Dougal waited for a moment, tried again, and moved along to the next shaft. It was identical to the first, and equally uncommunicative.

A methodical survey of the rest of the undercroft proved just as fruitless. Dougal had hoped for a doorway in the far corner on the courtyard side of the undercroft; for the builders of keep gatehouses had often worked to symmetrical designs. Doorway there was, but it was sealed with a recently constructed brick wall.

Dougal returned at length to his starting point, the trapdoor that led up to the gate passage. The two steel bars that held it in place were hinged at one end and secured at the other by a third bar, which acted as a

163

primitive bolt. One end of the latter bar ran into the stone of the vault; the other was retained by a steel staple that had been concreted into the ceiling.

The ladder beside the chute stretched invitingly from floor to ceiling. Dougal climbed a few rungs and ran his hand along the bar. It would move most easily from the center, if he grasped it at the point of balance. His hand curved round the cool metal, reminding Dougal of the feel of a javelin. He lifted it a fraction from the cradle of its staple and thrust it back. It ran smoothly for perhaps an inch and then refused to go any farther.

The salty taste of blood suddenly appeared in Dougal's mouth; he had bitten his lower lip. He jumped down and shifted the ladder until it was directly beneath the staple. The cause of the obstruction was immediately clear. A small, squat padlock, whose hasp passed through a hole drilled through the diameter of the cylindrical bar, had come to rest against the staple. He had not seen it before, since the bar had been twisted so the padlock was on the side away from the head of the ladder.

It was a simple lock, but solid and effective. Dougal tugged at both staple and padlock, in the vain hope that one of them would obligingly yield to his bare hands. He again took the risk of calling for Zelda. When there was no reply, he used the Webley to tap on the trapdoor.

The rhythm of his hammering—*short, short, short, long, long, long, short, short, short*—seemed to set up echoes all over the undercroft. The sound bounced back at him from all directions, like rapid small-arms fire.

Afterward, as the silence surrounded him again, he accepted what he had been trying to ignore since the lights first went off: the likelihood that Zelda and Malcolm were still at liberty belonged to the same order of probability as the likelihood that a blizzard had suddenly coated the castle and its environs with snow. Given the track record of British summers, Dougal would have given slightly shorter odds to the latter possibility. And he himself was responsible for whatever had happened to them. It was a shabby way to treat an old friend and someone who was rapidly becoming a new one.

Like small-arms fire . . .

Dougal stared down at the revolver, which he was still holding by the handle. He thought about the world of fiction, where people regularly shot the locks from doors; perhaps the doors were wooden. What effect would a bullet have against steel?

He climbed down the ladder, wiped his hands on his trousers, and stared up at the padlock. His eyes slid away, tracing a sample of the potentially lethal ricochets that a shot against metal might produce at such ludicrously short range in this confined space.

The pillar offered a little security, though less than it would have done if Dougal hadn't needed both hands to support the gun. He aligned the barrel with the padlock, swung the Webley down in a smooth arc, and squeezed the trigger.

The explosion, the whine of the bullet, the smack of metal on metal, and the duller but repeated concussions of metal on stone assaulted Dougal's ears without any discernible sequence. The kick of the Webley took

Dougal by surprise: it drove his bare forearm against the rough stone of the pillar.

The padlock hadn't moved. The light glinted on a blaze of brighter metal, a thin and shallow furrow that cut across the bar, perhaps an inch from the spot where the padlock dangled.

Not bad for a first attempt. Dougal moved slightly away from the pillar's shelter, trading a touch of security for a fractionally firmer stance.

The second shot was better: Dougal could sense it almost before the trigger reached its point of no return.

The explosion jogged another memory. For an instant, Dougal stared at the padlock without really taking in the small miracle that had occurred: the padlock, partially reduced to twisted metal, was now only connected to one end of its hasp; while he himself was completely undamaged.

But his attention was focused on the source of that technique of taking snapshots with a pistol. He could picture the sturdy figure of the schoolmaster who supervised Dougal's unwilling physical training during his teens; as a former regimental sergeant major, he also exercised a gentle but absolute despotism over the masters and pupils who made up the school's combined cadet force. Dougal visualized him squinting down the barrel of a rifle: "Nah, nah, Dougal, you may call yourself a pacifist, but you still got the strength to use a bloody pullthrough." The memories kept coming, with the speed and unpredictability of bullets.

The ex-RSM was in his inner sanctum, the school armory, flanked by racks of .303s and backed by a pile of ammunition boxes. The room had a characteristic smell of oil and metal.

Oil and metal.

Dougal lowered the revolver and stepped toward the ladder. Now why should the Gravers want to store weapons at Elmney Castle?

He climbed a few rungs, unhooked the remains of the padlock, and gently tugged the retaining bar from its socket. The two halves of the trapdoor, one after the other, swung downward; Dougal used his free hand to break their fall. They moved silently on well-oiled hinges. He was surprised by their weight—until he saw that their upper surfaces had been painstakingly coated with cobblestones in order to camouflage the trapdoor in the gatehouse passage. A faint evening breeze ruffled his hair.

Where the hell is Zelda?

As Dougal began to haul himself through the trapdoor, he became aware that something was terribly wrong. The main gates were still closed, but the postern was open. He could hear the soft snarl of a stationary engine out in the drive; the vehicle's headlamps rimmed the archway with light. The tunnel itself was empty.

Why hasn't Zelda rung the bell? Where's Malcolm?

Then sounds came out of the darkness beyond the headlights: gasps, the scuffing of gravel, and the chink of metal.

And Zelda's voice saying, "*Sheeit!*"

CHAPTER 15

Dougal burst through the postern into the forecourt. He was instantly blinded by the full beam of the headlamps: framed by the arch, he was at the mercy of whoever was in the darkness.

Instinctively, he dropped to the ground, sprawling full length and facedown on the gravel. He rolled out of the circle of light and tried to move round toward the sounds of the struggle. He was back on his feet, his fingers frantically searching for the Webley's safety catch, before he noticed that the sounds were retreating.

"Stop!" The shout emerged from Dougal's dry throat as a croak. The word hung futilely in the air behind him as he sprinted in pursuit of those fleeing footsteps.

The chase led him along the southern frontage of the castle toward the east tower, where Lady Graver was imprisoned. He called Zelda's name in his urgency to let her know that she was not alone. The need to reach her consumed his lesser preoccupations—the air rasping through his lungs, the stitch that stabbed deeper and deeper into his side, and the fear of hidden obstacles on this unfamiliar terrain.

The gravel sweep ended in a fence just beyond Lady Graver's tower. Dougal bruised his shins and ribs on a five-bar gate. The gate was ajar, which meant Zelda and her pursuer must have passed through it: no one would normally leave open a gate with sheep in the vicinity.

Dougal's eyes were beginning to adapt to the darkness. A long, walled kitchen garden, flanked by a line of greenhouses, stretched away from the castle. *Campernoyles Fruit & Vegetables?* He could hear the footsteps ahead. A door slammed, perhaps fifty yards away, and there was silence.

He wasted precious seconds searching for the doorway in a wall that was partly obscured with climbing plants. He found the door at last beside a clump of sweet-smelling honeysuckle. It led to a meadow whose deceptively smooth surface concealed ground caked hard by the drought and pockmarked with hoofprints. His ears caught the creak of rusty metal at the far end of the field: he sensed, rather than saw, two shadows scrambling one after the other through the fence and into the forest.

The fence was made of barbed wire. It tore Dougal's trousers; one barb sank deep into the palm of Dougal's right hand and scratched a jagged line of pain as he tried to pull it free. The butt of the Webley became warm and wet. He stood listening. For an instant, all he heard was the voice of that trim and enthusiastic RSM: "The butt of a Webley is designed to give a good grip. See how they grooved the surface? In the old days they used sharkskin on the hilts of swords. Same principle. Allows the sweat to drain away. And blood, of course."

The noises of the forest drowned the memory. Rustling leaves overlay sharper sounds that might possibly be snapping twigs and recoiling branches. They were out of sight, but not out of hearing.

He headed in the direction of the most distinct noises, willing himself to move slowly. He realized immediately that the forest on this side of the castle had little resemblance to the plantation of densely regular conifers through which he had reached the castle earlier in the day. These trees belonged to an era before the Forestry Commission had been invented—sprawling oaks and mature beeches, Dougal guessed, which grew without regimentation and with plenty of space between them. It made the going easier.

The logic of the hunt confined him, drawing him deeper into the trees. He lost track of time: his attention was wholly concentrated on that auditory will-o'-the-wisp in front of him. At times the sounds seemed all around him, as if a hundred people were escaping through the trees. His stitch and his tiredness vanished; he was conscious only of the forest around him and the gun in his hand.

Suddenly his quarry was nearer. He could hear beyond question two people struggling frantically through the undergrowth. He put on a spurt of speed. The ground dipped away from him and the shadows receded: he was in a clearing, a shallow depression ringed by trees like a sacrificial grove.

The ground shelved sharply away beneath his feet.

He caught a glimpse of two white shapes scurrying into the trees. His attention diverted, Dougal tripped. For a fragment of a second he had the illusion that he was flying—airborne on wings of adrenaline.

Ma-a-a-a . . .

As the lower part of Dougal's body splashed into the stream that unobtrusively bisected the clearing, the upper part fell against the stream's far bank with a jolt that winded him.

Two sheep. Two bloody terrified sheep.

He pulled himself painfully out of the stream. His ears automatically tracked the progress of the sheep: their flight became less urgent and then stopped; they must have lost interest in being hunted. He could hear no signs of Zelda or her assailant. Either they could both move with Red Indian stealth or they too had gone to ground.

Dougal sat heavily down on the bank and stifled a sob—out of caution, not manliness. Shivers rippled through his body. It was difficult to believe that a few hours ago he had been too hot. The night breeze ferreted out every cold, damp part of him and made them worse. He clasped his hands around his knees and briefly closed his eyes. The rustle of the leaves seemed to grow imperceptibly louder, as if the ancient trees around the clearing were muttering together as they converged on their latest victim.

It's just shock. Dougal forced open his eyes. The trees hadn't moved. *A natural reaction.* He diverted himself with practicalities: his boots and socks were waterlogged, but his trousers were drier than he had expected; the fall hadn't injured him, and the Webley had landed safely on dry, soft earth. He emptied the boots and wrung out the socks as best he could. The trousers could wait: a man without trousers was a man without defenses.

Defenses against what? Or whom?

Zelda's pursuer must be either Hanbury or Vertag; it was technically possible that a third party might have crawled out of the woodwork, but highly unlikely at this late stage in the proceedings. Probably Vertag, since he was expected. But in that case who had locked him in the cellar? Not Vertag, since he had only just arrived—the car engine and the headlights testified to that. That left Hanbury roaming about a place he had known since childhood, with Malcolm either unaware of his presence or already immobilized.

Dougal made a bid for calmness. If this were an academic problem, he would list the possible methods of solution. Having tabulated the options, he would choose that which his cool, trained mind told him was most likely to succeed. *Hell, twenty years of schooling must have some use.*

One, he could concentrate on saving his own skin and run away. The rational part of his mind applauded the elegant simplicity of this solution, but pointed out that he wouldn't get very far on foot at night in a large forest; and Malcolm had the car keys; besides, one had to give due weight to the wholly irrational consequences of abandoning two people who relied on you. Dougal regretfully conceded that there was little purpose in saving himself if he would be unable to live with himself afterward.

Two, he could stay where he was and wait for dawn

or his quarry to break cover—whichever happened first. This strategy would keep Dougal safe for the time being, but it would be of little help to Malcolm and Zelda. For all he knew, Zelda might be miles away by now.

Three, he could return to the castle. The advantages of this course, for others if not for himself, were immediately and depressingly obvious: Malcolm was there, whether or not he needed help; Zelda, if she was a free agent, would head back there; and it made sense in military terms to secure your base—particularly when the likes of Hanbury and Vertag might be about.

It had to be number three. The cool, trained mind was showing no signs of letting him off its hook.

At least the lie of the land was on his side. Since the castle and its park were on the top of the spur of the hills, all Dougal had to do was to go up rather than down.

He moved cautiously out of the clearing and was delighted to find that he had hit a path; he would be able to move more quickly and quietly without the fear of rustling undergrowth. On the other hand, every step he made in his waterlogged boots was accompanied by a soft but perfectly audible squelch.

After twenty paces Dougal could no longer bear to listen to himself. The sound of his feet swelled in his mind until it could have drowned a goose-stepping regiment of giants in soggy jackboots. He stopped, listened, and bent down to unlace his boots. He would try wringing out the socks again. If that failed he would carry the boots round his neck.

Just as he slipped off his right boot, a movement

displaced the air above his head. He whipped round, one hand raised to ward off attack, the other reaching for the gun.

He was too late. His attention was wholly diverted by a pain that flowered with sudden violence beside his left ear. The pain grew like a well-fertilized weed. Its tendrils swiftly obliterated his head and then blotted out the rest of the universe.

CHAPTER 16

Nothingness gave way to pain. Pain gradually became a sea studded with islands of awareness. The sea receded to create continents. When the sea was no more than a puddle, Dougal touched his head.

The bump was covered with matted hair, tacky with blood. Dougal groaned. With infinite care he moved each of his limbs in turn.

It took him several attempts to succeed in sitting up. The achievement was marred by waves of nausea. As the swell subsided, Dougal became obsessed by the question of time. Other questions, such as who or what had hit him, were imponderable in his present condition.

The blood on his scalp was coagulating: he must have been unconscious for more than a few seconds. But there was no sign of dawn in the sky. Ten minutes? A couple of hours?

There was nothing for it but to continue the journey back to the castle. Dougal felt incapable of assessing the implications of the attack. When there was nothing else to stick to, you might as well stick to the last decision you could remember making.

His departure was delayed while he searched for the Webley and his missing boot. He found them at last in a clump of nettles. Dougal licked the burning patches on his hands. The clump was at least two yards away from where he had fallen and behind the spot where his attacker must have stood. That argued that his assailant must already be armed, probably with a gun as well as with a malign sense of humour.

Dougal followed the path uphill. This time, he lacked the energy to take precautions: all his efforts were concentrated on staying upright and moving.

Perhaps the exercise helped. By the time the path arrived at a gate in the park fencing, at a spot a few hundred yards south of the kitchen garden wall, Dougal felt as normal as it was possible to be when one had a savage headache, bruised limbs, no cigarettes, and an overwhelming lack of confidence in the future. He slipped through the gate and stared across the meadow at the facade of the castle.

The east wing, where Lady Graver had been (and perhaps still was) confined, was in darkness. The car belonging to Zelda's pursuer was no longer in front of the gatehouse. There was a row of lights along the windows of the first floor of the west wing; Dougal could make out the big bay of the library.

Dougal picked his way across the sheep-cropped grass toward the gatehouse. The only sign of life was a faint thudding—a series of blows that seemed to emanate with pulselike regularity from the west wing. The noise increased in volume as Dougal reached the gravel.

It sounded as if someone with a sledgehammer had taken a violent dislike to the castle.

Sacrificing caution to speed, Dougal forced his aching body into a run. The thudding continued unabated as he reached the shelter of the gateway. The main gates had been pulled back. The tunnel beyond was empty. The trapdoor once again concealed the entrance to the undercroft.

Dougal advanced through the tunnel and made a slow circuit of the courtyard. A Ford Sierra, its bonnet still warm, was parked beside the east wing. A quick glimpse around the interior revealed nothing but a folder of information for those who rent cars from Hertz. The keys were gone and the boot was locked.

The rest of the courtyard, as far as Dougal could tell, was unchanged and uninhabited. The house was another matter altogether. As soon as Dougal stepped into the brightly lit hall, the hammering became louder and far more menacing. His eyes struggled to adjust to the light. He had been close to panic in the darkness outside; but the eerie normality of the hall, together with those deafening blows, brought him still closer.

He licked his lips, which felt as if they had been chapped by a sandstorm, and climbed the stairs toward the source of the banging.

In a few seconds, he was outside the library. The door was made of a heavy redwood. One of its upper panels was vibrating under the force of the blows behind it. A crack running along the grain of the wood opened and closed in time with the hammering. After each thud came a snarling grunt.

Dougal backed away. If Vertag and Zelda were still

in the forest, the enraged prisoner within the Gravers' library would be either Hanbury or Malcolm. Unless, of course, someone had decided to give Joe or his father a change of scene.

The rhythm was broken by the sound of splintering wood. An oblong gap in the panel appeared. Dougal was amazed to see that the head of an eagle was protruding from the hole; the bird was attacking the wood beneath his beak in a manner that suggested it harbored a secret ambition to be a woodpecker.

The eagle withdrew and the hole became slightly larger. Dougal watched as a brawny arm snaked through the jagged opening and dived down toward the door handle.

"Damn it," said Malcolm. "The bastard's taken the key."

The smell of coffee hung heavily on the night air. The Gravers went in for a fine Tanzanian blend, which was something to be said in their favor. Waiting for the coffee to cool, Dougal lined up four aspirins beside his mug.

". . . I was over the other side of the room beside the safe. I heard nothing until the door banged. Then the lock clicked. My first thought was to get the Colt, but it was gone: I'd left it on that little wine table by the door."

Malcolm paused as he fed the last round into the Webley. Dougal had been forced to empty the gun before the lock on the library had given way. Malcolm raised the gun, aimed across the courtyard, and pretended to pull the trigger. *Pow!* Dougal managed to swallow two of the aspirins with a mouthful of scalding coffee.

"The window was out: even if I could have squeezed through, I didn't fancy the drop. There's a railing underneath like a row of spears. So that left the door. I smashed a chair on it first. Then I found the mace in one of the cupboards. You know what it says on the handle? *Made in Birmingham.* Typical of this bloody place. Victorian kitsch. Still, at least it has a bit of weight, and that eagle's head got through the door in the end. . . . Are you okay?"

Dougal shrugged. He preferred not to put how he felt into words. "Tense," he conceded. "A bit tired."

They were sitting on a stone bench a few yards from the front door. Malcolm had taken Dougal's refusal to leave without Zelda very well. Now, all they could do was wait. Their position covered the two ways into the castle—through the gatehouse and among the ruins of the north wall. Dougal was relieved that Malcolm had taken back the Webley.

Malcolm fumbled in one of the pockets of his uniform tunic. "What you need is a joint. That'll relax you."

"For God's sake," Dougal snapped. "That's the last thing I need."

"Some speed then?" Malcolm dug into another pocket. "A little snort of amphetamine sulphate would soon perk you up. . . . Oh, all right. Sorry I spoke. You're in one of your not-tonight-Josephine moods, aren't you?"

Dougal swilled the last of the coffee round his mouth to remove the taste of the aspirin. He felt quite drugged

179

enough already: his skin was clammy, his breathing swift and shallow, and the coffee had made him queasy.

It might help if he concentrated on something else. "We'd better trade information while we can. The gatehouse undercroft has recently been turned into a warehouse, with access for the goods via a trapdoor in the tunnel. Nice and quiet for loading and unloading. It's empty now, but there's a smell of oil and metal down there which somehow reminded me of—"

"Guns." Malcolm grinned. "Go on, I'll fill you in later."

"There's not much more. Someone turned out the light and locked me in. All I saw was a glimpse of blue. Not your blue—more like jeans. I shot the padlock off the trapdoor and got out that way. A car—that Sierra—had just arrived, and its driver and Zelda were fighting on the gravel. He chased Zelda into the forest and I followed. I think I was chasing a couple of sheep for most of the time. I was heading back to you when someone jumped on me and knocked me out. When I got back here, the only sign of life was you battering down the door. But someone had moved the Sierra into the courtyard and shut the trapdoor."

"And you reckon it was Vertag in the car and Hanbury wandering round the castle?"

Dougal nodded. "It's not certain, of course. But whoever locked us in must have known the place well— he knew where to find the library key, for instance. As far as we know, Vertag's never been here before."

"Why didn't Zelda retreat into the castle when she saw the car coming up the drive?"

"That worried me. The most likely thing is that her

retreat was or seemed to be cut off. Maybe she saw Hanbury coming through the front door—he must have been around somewhere. Or maybe it was the noise of me trying to get through the trapdoor. Remember, I fired two shots more or less under her feet. Either way, she panicked and ran outside."

Malcolm chuckled. "She didn't do too badly. She may be on the run, but at least she escaped. And she had the .22 with her—it isn't on the gravel."

"I hope so." Dougal sighed. "Hanbury might have picked it up when he moved the Sierra. Oh, hell. As he's not in the castle now, he's probably joined the midnight ramble in the forest."

"Don't worry," said Malcolm unexpectedly. "That young woman is a survivor." He raised his coffee mug in a silent toast. "So. Vertag's after Zelda in the forest; Hanbury is trying to find them both; and we can expect Zelda to come back here whether she's a free agent or . . . or a captive."

"That's it." The aspirins were beginning to work. Dougal rubbed a finger along the haft of the mace. "When Zelda gets back, we go as quickly as possible. Have you done the cars?"

"I thought we'd use the Volvo. It's all ready to go with the keys in the ignition. No one will be using the Range Rover or the Sierra until they've been extensively rewircd. My suitcase is here."

Malcolm bent down and patted a dark oblong beneath the bench.

"What have you got?"

"Mainly stuff from the safe. The good news was that it contained a nice little nest egg—all used notes, mainly in sterling. Probably around thirty to forty grand." He pulled the suitcase out. In the faint, predawn light, Dougal could see that its lid was bulging like a boil on the verge of breaking.

"Is that all you've got in there?"

"Lady Graver had a little antique jewelry . . . and I couldn't resist one or two small bits of silver. There was a lovely little Queen Anne tea canister in the dining room. But the really interesting thing is this."

Malcolm eased back the catches of the suitcase. The lid flew back. "Take a look." He handed Dougal a torch and two transparent plastic folders.

Carefully shielding the light, Dougal flicked through the contents of the folders. One contained a photocopy of a typed list of addresses, covering five sheets of paper. The addresses belonged to private individuals in Britain, the United States, Holland, West Germany, and Ireland—on both sides of the border. He recognized none of them and said so.

Malcolm pointed to one on the second sheet: "Albert Curran, 45A Yorktown Place, London NW1."

"NW1 is the postal district for Camden Town. I think Yorktown Place is a couple of blocks behind Campernoyles. Albert could very easily be Fat Bert."

Dougal grunted and picked up the other folder. It held another list, this time of items and prices, quoted in U. S. dollars with attractive discounts on bulk purchases. "Skorpion VZ61 . . . Armalite AR18 . . . Heckler & Koch MP5 . . . Uzi . . . Kalashnikov AK47 . . ." The selection was by no means confined to guns, though most items were portable. The range extended to surface-to-air missiles.

The list filled two and a half sides. There was the occasional comment: "extremely effective in crowds, but replacement parts may be difficult to obtain" or "reliability guaranteed by extensive combat trials in the Falklands."

"A mail order catalogue?" Dougal passed the folders back to Malcolm, hoping the quiver in his voice wasn't too obvious.

"So it seems. Goods stored in the undercroft. Campernoyles Fruit & Veg vans coming and going. A beautiful cover, with the bonus that Graver's a JP: he may be dotty, but he's the last person the police would interfere with. Not in Gloucestershire."

"And the list of addresses would be customers? Middlemen? Who is running the whole affair?" Dougal paused to consider the last question. Not the Gravers: they would never have initiated something like this, though someone had clearly bribed and bullied them into providing a service. Hanbury might well have made the arrangements—he knew the Gravers and their financial position, but he was a broker of crime who would surely be unwilling to be constantly and actively involved in arms smuggling itself.

Vertag. It was even logical, Dougal supposed, that the chief executive of the Sealed Servants of the Apocalypse should be making money by arming potential combatants at Armageddon.

"There's something else you should notice." Malcolm nudged the folders back toward Dougal. "Not the message this time. The medium."

Dougal stared blankly, first at the papers, then at Malcolm.

"When I was enjoying my enforced holiday," Malcolm continued, "your letters were quite important. I read them rather a lot. I counted the spelling mistakes. I even analyzed your damn syntax. I could recognize your letters as soon as I saw the envelope: by the typeface. Hell, William, you're meant to be the paleographer."

The academic training that had lain submerged in Dougal's mind for sixth months floated unwillingly to the surface. The typeface of the shopping list and the addresses was the same: elite, at a guess, with twelve characters to an inch; the loops of the *e*'s were blocked; the tip of the ascender of the *b* was missing; the *l*'s tended to be followed by their shadow. The type probably belonged to a middle-aged portable in need of servicing.

Not unlike the Remington ii gathering dust in his West Hampstead flat.

Malcolm nodded. "It's yours, all right. I'd swear to it. My bet is that someone's been busy acquiring circumstantial evidence in your absence. Must be Hanbury."

"They can do tests," Dougal protested. "No typist uses the same combinations of pressure on the keys as another. Not an amateur on a manual."

"These are photocopies, and not very good quality. I doubt if they're clear enough for an expert to use." Malcolm tapped the folders with a stubby forefinger: "These aren't the coffin itself: just a few nails to help hold it together."

"They wouldn't stand up in a court of law."

"Maybe the idea is that you wouldn't either."

The calculation was so easy that neither of them needed to say the answer aloud: *blood sacrifice*. Postmortem possibilities, hybrids of reasoning and intuition, rumbled into Dougal's mind like a regiment of tanks.

His death might be presented as an accident or as the result of infighting between criminal or terrorist factions. It didn't matter. The important thing was that his body should trigger a methodical police investigation into the circumstances that led to his death. They would run a routine check on Scotland Yard's computer records. That would establish that, although he had no criminal record, he was a known associate of those who had; he was an inhabitant of that gray area between crime and respectability. The Inland Revenue and the Department of Health and Social Security would be only too glad to confirm his dubious status in society.

The police would uncover his unexplained income and his erratic movements. Then, of course, they would be fed with more specific items of information. The photocopies were just one example—Hanbury could be trusted to do a thorough job.

"Dead men," said Malcolm with a certain relish that Dougal found wholly unnecessary, "don't tell lies— and they don't answer questions either. If you ask me, Vertag and the Gravers hired your fat friend to create an illusion. A diversion. A body leads to a paper chase. A few redundant weapons, perhaps. It all adds up to an arms business, just like the whisper said there was. But now as dead as its proprietor. P. C. Plod and his

185

team marvel at their acumen and bugger off home. And Elmney slumbers undisturbed. Not even a trial. Can you think of a better theory?"

"Why did they run the risk of kidnapping Zelda?"

"To keep you on a leash, of course. And they were right about that, weren't they? I expect she'll also play a supporting role as subsidiary corpse."

Dougal tightened his grip on the mace and wondered what would happen if he brought the eagle's beak down on Hanbury's head. Blood? A jellylike gray matter?

"I'd like to set a match to this whole bloody mausoleum, with all of them inside it."

"Can do," said Malcolm enthusiastically. "Lots of spare petrol in the garage and a fire would spread very quickly in this breeze."

"Don't be stupid."

Malcolm grinned. "I'd spare Joe. I fancy him something rotten."

"I know. You can send him a postcard tomorrow. Better still, say it with flowers."

But Malcolm's attention was elsewhere. He silenced Dougal with a nudge. The sound of footsteps reached them: the crunching of gravel outside the gatehouse gave way to the crisp echoes of the tunnel. There were two people, Dougal realized, and one of them was talking.

He and Malcolm were already on their feet, edging into the shadows beyond the bench. Dougal caught his breath as Hanbury and Zelda emerged into the courtyard. They were absorbed in a conversation that sounded suspiciously like a squabble.

". . . better things to do than tramp around the coun-

tryside at night," Hanbury was saying. "Your ineffi-
ciency appalls me."

Zelda said something inaudible, which had the effect
of making Hanbury still more petulant.

"Yes, what about it? You leave human debris strewn
over a large part of southern England, all to no purpose,
and expect *me* to clear it up. Let me tell you—"

The slam of the front door cut off the rest of Hanbury's words. Dougal put his mouth close to Malcolm's
ear: "Wait till they're upstairs. Then we'll take Hanbury, one on each side. I'll try to get between him
and Zelda. He's quite capable of using her as a shield."

"Or vice versa."

"What?"

"For God's sake, William. Weren't you listening?
Zelda's in it as much as he is."

CHAPTER 17

"If you open the door of that cupboard on the left of the fireplace," Hanbury said with the air of a man trying hard to be helpful in adverse circumstances, "we could all have a drink. Aunt Matilda includes a love of single malts among her many vices."

Malcolm looked at Dougal, his eyebrows raised.

Dougal pulled the heavy red velvet curtains across the window and turned.

"Can we trust them?" He nodded toward Hanbury and Zelda, side by side on the sofa. "They're probably planning to use their glasses as offensive weapons."

"Believe me, William," said Hanbury, craning his head round so that he could see Dougal at the edge of his field of vision, "I do sympathize with your very natural feeling of bitterness. But don't let it cloud your judgment. It's true that Zelda and I could throw our glasses at you. But we would probably miss, given the constraints of our present position. Anyway, what would be the point? We couldn't follow through. It would be entirely counterproductive: you would feel even more irritated with us, and we would have deprived ourselves of a glass of excellent whisky."

For once Hanbury was demonstrably speaking the truth. His right wrist was linked to Zelda's left with the handcuffs Malcolm had briefly used on Graver. They were sitting on the sofa, which like the armchairs was not easy to escape from at the best of times. Malcolm had devoted some time, much ingenuity, and the rest of the ball of twine to their ankles. Hanbury's right ankle was lashed to Zelda's left; their other ankles were tied to the massive oak legs of the sofa itself. Their posture wasn't elegant, but it was undoubtedly secure.

It was a three-seater sofa. Dougal squashed the rebellious feeling of relief that Zelda wasn't wearing a skirt. It was ridiculous to care about her dignity at this juncture. Hanbury's dignity, on the other hand, was untouched. The handcuffs were an amusing accessory to the rest of his elaborately casual attire. He wore a pair of jeans and a denim jacket, both of which bore the label of a French designer, and the sort of shirt that clings to the chest of the more sartorially fastidious lumberjack.

"Well?" Malcolm asked.

Dougal crossed the library to the fireplace. The cupboard was recessed into the paneling. "*I'm* going to have a drink. I suppose we might as well let them have one too. It might loosen their tongues."

The contents of the cupboard bore witness to the seriousness with which Lady Graver took her vices. Brandy, gin, and other spirits were adequately represented; but the range of whiskies would have put most

189

off-licenses to shame. The gleaming ranks of several dozen brands stretched back into the dark depths of the cupboard.

Hanbury chuckled. "Impressive, eh? The Highland malts are on the left; the Lowland, Islay, and so forth are on the right. I'd appreciate some Lagavulin, if you can put your hand on it."

Dougal was about to ignore the request when he noticed the Lagavulin in front of him. It seemed churlish to deny it to Hanbury. The glasses and bottled water from Loch Katrine were on the shelf above. Malcolm chose a Glenlivet and Zelda followed suit; she refused to look up, and Dougal was uneasily aware that her cheeks were wet.

He himself picked the squat-bottled Jura malt.

Hanbury nodded approvingly. "An interesting choice. Unusually delicate for an Island whisky. I think it's underrated, myself. Of course, it hasn't been back on the market for very long—"

"James." Dougal spoke quietly but with a savagery that surprised him. "Will you shut up? You can have a drink, but I'm damned if you're going to talk about malts all night."

He sat down in the armchair beside the cupboard, resting the Webley on the arm. Malcolm stayed on his feet behind the sofa, gun in one hand and drink in the other.

The spirit glided down Dougal's throat, easing the trembling that had been with him since he found Zelda on the edge of the forest. He had intended to ask Malcolm for a cigarette, but now decided to leave it until he had finished his drink.

190

The first drink. He wanted to swim in the bloody stuff.

Hanbury stayed silent. He fished out a perfectly laundered handkerchief and dabbed his scalp. Dougal's blow with the back of the mace had broken the skin.

Dougal fought back the urge to yawn. The evening had a long way to go before it was over. He looked up at Malcolm.

"How are we fixed?" he asked.

"Everything's under control," Malcolm said. "All the gates and outside doors are locked. The Gravers are awake and healthy, though rather grumpy. I got the Volvo out and left it in the courtyard."

"Good. Once we've got a few answers, we'll be off."

"You deserve some answers," Hanbury said. "Heaven knows, it hasn't been easy for me to keep you in the dark for so long. The root of the problem was a conflict of loyalties. I underestimated your abilities again, too. I should have been frank from the start."

Dougal ignored the flattery. It wasn't due to him but to the gun beside him. Malcolm and luck had saved him from being in a worse position than Hanbury's; good judgment had nothing to do with it.

Good judgment had nothing to do with falling in love with a woman who was privately conspiring to kill him. It hadn't been love, of course—just a passing fancy based on a brief acquaintance. Dougal drained his glass and poured himself another.

"With your permission," Hanbury continued, "I'll begin with Vertag. The rest of us bear the same relationship as the lesser planets to the sun. Shall I proceed?"

"Go on. But you can cut out the ornate metaphors."

The whisky was already doing its work. The trembling had stopped. Dougal's mind was working again—though whether it was capable of handling the conversational contortions of James Hanbury was quite another matter.

"Alex Vertag isn't exactly a criminal." Hanbury spoke softly, as if Vertag was listening in the next room. "He's an idealist. You remember all those enthusiasms that burgeoned in the sixties? The age of Aquarius and so on? That's when he got involved with a New York–based doomsday group. They hoped to avert the impending global catastrophe by good intentions. The group collapsed, but Vertag went on to found the Sealed Servants. But the SSA has a very different emphasis: it's not trying to avoid or publicize the end of the world as we know it—instead it's trying to get the best possible terms of survival for its membership. Its thinking is fundamentally fascist: we are the chosen people and sod the rest. And the SSA is well organized and surprisingly wealthy. Vertag may be a crank, but he was educated at Harvard Business School.

"The SSA is entirely legitimate. But Vertag himself carries the logic a little farther than his comrades. For him, the end justifies the means: it's better for humanity in the long run to make a profit from hastening the old world to its end than to try to save it. The SSA is his version of Noah's ark—with himself as Noah. The more money he has, the better the ark's chance of survival."

"You're just saying he's a crook who believes himself to be a public benefactor." This time Dougal offered the others a refill of whisky as well. "Speed it up, will you?"

Hanbury acknowledged the reproof with a wave of his glass. "He started with drugs—mainly cocaine and the opiates; there's been little profit in hallucinogens recently. That gave him contacts with several East Coast crime syndicates and some of the less scrupulous revolutionary groups. It all led him quite naturally to the arms trade.

"I ran into him about three years ago. He kept a very low profile, but our interests overlapped and I wanted to make sure there was no conflict. We were able to do one another a few good turns. I've never *liked* the man, you understand, but he has an excellent business brain."

"One good turn was to introduce him to the Gravers?"

"That's right, William. My motive was altruistic, I confess. I've known the Graver family all my life— Elmney was one of my childhood haunts. Lady Graver was like a mother to me. I couldn't just stand by and let poor Thos drift into bankruptcy. One has one's responsibilities. I knew Vertag wanted a reliable British base for his, ah, transport business. It was a heaven-sent opportunity."

"And a heaven-sent commission for you as well?"

"Well, in a manner of speaking. Aunt Matilda insisted. If you want to do business with friends, she said, you have to keep it on a businesslike footing."

Dougal's fingers tightened round his glass. "James, you pulled those three innocents into the international arms trade, okay? There's nothing altruistic in lining your own pockets by supporting terrorism without any risk to yourself. As usual, you left the risks to your friends."

"You judge me harshly, William. And perhaps justly." Hanbury looked directly at Dougal, his eyes sad and compelling. "I made a tragic mistake and believe me I am paying for it."

"Balls," said Malcolm behind the sofa.

"You're coming on too strong, James," said Zelda. The sound of her voice, after her long silence, came as a physical shock to Dougal. "Just stick to the facts, right? These guys don't want to know your human angle."

"But it's the truth!" Hanbury seemed genuinely shocked by his reception. "Why should I lie to you?"

"I don't know," Dougal said. "Lack of reason never stopped you before."

"Well, it's true that I had my doubts about Vertag. There are criminals and criminals, you know." Hanbury drew a Gauloise from the pocket of his shirt and lit it with a wafer-thin gold lighter. "But I only became aware of his less desirable qualities and the scope of his, ah, antisocial activities after I had introduced him to the Gravers. It's not an important point"—Hanbury's tone was that of a psychiatrist humoring a truculent patient—"but Zelda will confirm it. After all, it was she who removed many of the scales from my eyes."

"What do you mean?" Dougal set down his glass on the arm of his chair and rested his hand on the Webley.

Hanbury's smile was as tranquil as the peace that

passes all understanding. "I'm afraid this will irritate you still further. I've known Zelda for some time—a business relationship, of course. Information is a commodity like any other, and I have contacts in areas where commerce tends to be restricted. A good broker will always find a suitable buyer."

Dougal looked at Zelda, while Hanbury leaned back with the comfortable expression of a penitent who has just redirected the wrath of God to a more deserving sinner.

"All right," Dougal said at last. "It's truth time. Who are you?"

"I didn't lie to you, honey," she said, so softly that Dougal could hardly hear. "It's just I didn't tell you the whole story."

"Shall I say it for you?" Hanbury inquired solicitously. He turned back to Dougal. "Zelda has a unique position in America. She's a sop to feminism and race relations. Not to put too fine a point on it, she works for the covert operations division of the CIA."

CHAPTER 18

The qualities of silences vary; some are as light as a feather duvet, while others are more like a slab of concrete. When Dougal broke the stillness that followed Hanbury's announcement, his words sounded like the blows of a sledgehammer.

"Why should we believe you this time? Either of you?"

"Call the U. S. Embassy in London. They don't officially know I'm here, but if you ask for extension 2503 they'll confirm my accreditation. Mention my name and say it's an identification under section B23. The number's—"

"Don't tell us," Dougal said. "I think we'd better get it from directory inquiries."

The silence returned while Malcolm left the room to use the telephone in the hall. Zelda wanted to speak, but Dougal shook his head. Both she and Hanbury had deceived him with words, and he preferred to wait for Malcolm to return. Malcolm was not just a witness; he was an anchor to objectivity.

If Hanbury and Zelda were old associates, then Hanbury must have engineered the meeting on Rhodes. How much of Dougal's life had Hanbury arranged? Dougal had never felt that he had much control over his private life, but he objected very strongly to someone taking over the job on his behalf. Probably a youthful Hanbury had been hovering over the marital bed of Dougal's parents at the very moment when Dougal was conceived.

He realized that the whisky was getting to him. He put his empty glass on the floor by the chair, beyond easy reach of temptation.

At that moment, Malcolm slipped back into the library.

"She's real," he said. "Or at least someone on the other end of the line says she is."

"Good. We'll continue. Not you, James. Zelda."

She rubbed her temples with her free hand. "If I don't, James will. What do you guys want me to say? I'm just one of the indians. One of the agency's tame sources for information science. Sure, I'm on the covert operations payroll—it's bureacratically convenient, and I guess they figure my sex and color make good natural cover. They're *real*, like my whole college career. I go round the international conference circuit and provide the agency with deep background material. Most of it is straight reporting—anyone could do the job by scanning a dozen journals. I'm also meant to listen in to what Herr X says to Natasha Y over the third martini, but X and Y tend to have better heads for alcohol than me."

"So how did Hanbury enter your blameless little

life?" Malcolm's disbelief was as evident as the henna in his hair, glinting in the overhead light.

Zelda tried to twist her head toward him; it was too painful, so her eyes returned to Dougal. "Occasionally they want me to get hold of a hunk of hardware. Usually the Eastern bloc's latest copy of an American microtech design. Someone at our Prague station suggested trying James in London. They say he goes shopping for several intelligence agencies. That's how we met. I've used him maybe three or four times."

"You're just small-fry, like the rest of us?" Dougal addressed the bottom of his empty glass. "If you are, what are you doing here?"

"Because I'm such a small fish that I'm practically invisible—that's one reason. Look, Vertag has the agency real scared. Okay, drugs and arms are all in a day's work. What worries them is that Vertag is moving into freelance espionage. They've got evidence that Vertag has a lot of buddies at Langley itself. You know how paranoid security services are these days—they spend more time looking for leaks than for information. First I knew of it was when my section head set up a meeting in this godforsaken motel. When I got there, I found he'd brought the director along for the ride. Can you imagine it? They gave me this heavy stuff about patriotism and how I had to save America. Then they mentioned Vertag as a target for priority executive action under the CE ruling. They'd volunteered me for the job."

Common Entrance? Church of England? Chief Engineer?

Dougal's lack of comprehension must have shown in his face. Zelda gave him the ghost of a smile.

"Sorry. CE stands for Compulsory Elimination. They chose me because the regular channels were suspect; they couldn't be sure that Vertag hadn't hired himself someone in the executive section. I'm an outsider—I don't think anyone outside of my section head even knows of my existence. What they didn't say is that they could afford to sling me overboard if I blew it. And I guess that choosing me must have given my section head a whole lot of fun. He's a Texas redneck, and black women who stray outside of the cotton fields make him feel kind of *weird* inside."

Dougal restrained a grin with difficulty. "Your selection still sounds as plausible as a bacon sandwich in the Blue Mosque."

"The clincher was the fact I know James. That's why I got the motel civics course rather than one of the other little fishes. Their original idea was to plant a little coke on Vertag and arrest him in New York. But the FBI blew it, or maybe Vertag heard a whisper. He was out of the country before anyone realized what had happened. Out of sight and beyond our jurisdiction. The director's computer figured Vertag would go to ground in Europe. It also analyzed Vertag's European connections and rated them according to information potential and motivational flexibility. James got the highest grades on both lists."

"I can't think why," said Hanbury plaintively. "Still, if one has to be ranked, one likes to be ranked first."

Zelda ignored him. "And James was my contact, though I knew him in a very different context. On this side of the Atlantic, he's the only known associate of Vertag's who isn't a licensed freak. At least you know where you are with him. So I was told to lean on James until he found out where Vertag was, and then do the CE. You with me so far?"

"I follow you," Dougal said, "but the only reason to believe you is that it sounds so ridiculous. Surely your employers could have found a better way of getting rid of Vertag?"

"Sweetheart, you need to remember how jumpy the CIA has gotten about killing people. Especially U. S. citizens. If they went through standard agency procedures to get Vertag, they'd either use their own people or put out a contract in the underworld. Either way, a whole lot more people might get to hear about it. They needed me in any case, for tracing James, so it made sense of a sort to use me for the whole operation."

"Supposing we accept that," Malcolm said behind her. "You approached Hanbury and got him to lead you to Vertag. Why drag us into it?"

"Ah," Hanbury said, "that was my idea. I really had no choice." Hanbury's voice lowered its pitch. "I imagine that all of us here accept that Vertag is dangerous? His death is a matter of some urgency, which, ah, transcends considerations of personal gain or national interest. Naturally I wanted to help Zelda, but I was drastically handicapped by the fact that Vertag had heard a whisper of my connection with the CIA. I believe I mentioned that when we met at the Café Royal. Vertag would hardly send me a postcard with his new forwarding address. The only way I could help Zelda was through my link with the Gravers. The Gravers are old friends, but I couldn't afford to be open with them because I knew poor Joe was infatuated with Vertag. No, the one foolproof method to bring Vertag into the open was to create an emergency that necessitated his personal attention. Which is why I mentioned to our hosts that Fat Bert was a police informer."

"Was he?" Dougal asked.

"Of course not. But he's the sort of person who might well have been. I sent him some cash anonymously through the post to reinforce the impression—I knew he would spend it at once in such a surreptitious way that everyone would notice. The Gravers, of course, panicked and sent for Vertag, using whatever emergency communication channel he had provided them with. It wasn't a perfect plan, I know, but it was the only way I could think of to flush Vertag out of hiding."

Dougal could bear it no longer. He stood up. His options were, in order of preference, to hit Hanbury, to steal one of his cigarettes, or to have some more whisky. He chose the whisky.

He poured three fingers into his glass. "You must have known what would happen to Bert."

Hanbury shrugged. "The bleating of the kid, my dear William. You're not suggesting that one should leave the tiger on the rampage?"

"You still haven't explained why you found it necessary to involve me. Between you, surely you and the CIA could have traced and dealt with Vertag?"

"In normal circumstances, yes." Hanbury lit another cigarette. "But not in these. We knew that Vertag would run a mile if he caught so much as a whiff of me; the CIA has hamstrung itself. And we knew that the Gravers were—are—unreliable. So I thought of you. I knew I might need a round-the-clock check on Vertag's movements in this country, so I could bring him and Zelda together at the appropriate moment. Besides, I was glad to have the opportunity of doing you a good turn. The CIA pays very well by European standards, you know."

There was a hint of truth here, Dougal thought, lurking behind a protective screen of prevarication. Suppose Hanbury was under pressure from Zelda to produce Vertag, it would be only natural for him to want someone else to take the risks.

But the rest of the truth was still missing. Extracting information from Hanbury was like getting a walnut from its shell; you expected to lose a lot in the process.

Dougal stood up, prevented himself from swaying by an effort of will, and walked across to the suitcase on the other side of the fireplace. Malcolm's eyes followed him.

The lid of the suitcase bounced back. Dougal pulled out a couple of jewel boxes and assorted silverware and found the two folders.

He threw them onto Hanbury's lap. "These suggest you had a rather more sophisticated role in mind for me."

Hanbury flipped them onto the carpet. "You misunderstand, William. I know these papers might suggest we were trying to frame you. But they were merely intended to establish your bona fides with the Gravers. How else do you think I could persuade Joe to recommend you to Vertag?"

"So both Vertag and the Gravers were led to believe

I was a professional killer? And if anything went wrong, I could carry the can?"

"Quite." Hanbury beamed. "You're there at last. Really rather witty. Joe was able to present you to Vertag in your dual role as executioner and scapegoat—and say it was all his own idea. You've got to realize how much that boy wanted to earn Vertag's approval."

"And I suppose if something had gone wrong with your arrangements for Vertag's demise—" Dougal began—

"No, William, no! You have my word that those papers were merely intended to camouflage the real reason for your presence to the Gravers and Vertag. They were never meant for use—I would hate you to get the wrong impression."

Hanbury's brow was furrowed with worry. He projected, with an almost physical force, the idea that Dougal's opinion of him was the most important thing in the world. The effect of his gaze had nothing to do with reason, but it was undeniably powerful. The effect on its victim's critical faculties was analogous to that of a tin of condensed milk on the taste buds.

Dougal started to rummage through the suitcase again—anything to escape the appeal in those terrible eyes. He took out everything except the currency.

"What are you doing?" Malcolm asked.

"We don't need all this. It'll be hard to dispose of and it's not worth that much." Dougal's fingers strayed over a large polyethylene freezer bag, sealed with a twist of wire. "What's this?"

"Ah," said Malcolm, "I was going to mention that. It was under Joe's mattress."

203

Dougal unwound the wire and upturned the bag. Several dozen smaller bags scattered onto the floor. Their contents were white, shrouded in plastic wrap and yielded to the touch.

"It seems that heroin was Joe's little subsidiary." Malcolm grinned broadly. "I reckon there's twenty or thirty ounces there. Break it down to gram deals and it'll be worth more than the cash. Though it's probably safe to flog it in bulk lots and leave the street risks to others."

"No. We don't want it."

"But you can't just chuck away a fortune like that." Malcolm didn't sound angry—merely incredulous.

"He's right, you know," Hanbury said. "It would be a criminal waste of an extremely valuable commodity. You could leave it with me if you two would rather avoid the additional complications."

Malcolm and Hanbury spoke for several minutes. It was an unlikely alliance, Dougal thought, the more so because neither of them was entirely moved by personal greed. To his surprise he realized that they were both profoundly shocked by his failure to capitalize on a perfectly good asset. Dougal was breaking the first—and possibly the only—commandment of their Darwinian code.

He turned his back on them, and on their arguments, and crouched by the fireplace. He methodically twisted the papers from the safe and piled them in the grate. He added a layer of kindling from a dusty bundle at one end of the hearth and completed the pyramid with an apex of plastic bags. Heroin must be combustible: you could smoke it.

"You disappoint me, William," said Hanbury, as Dougal took his lighter from the arm of the sofa.

Malcolm was silent now, but Zelda gave Dougal a quick encouraging nod.

"You don't for one moment believe that there's any point in what you're doing? It won't mean one fewer junkie around Piccadilly Circus. You can't treat a symptom without dealing with the cause." Hanbury moved forward in his agitation, and Malcolm automatically tapped a warning on the already damaged part of his scalp.

A tongue of flame licked round one corner of the pyramid. Dougal lit the opposite corner and sat back on his heels. Thick blue smoke was sucked up the wide chimney. Dougal envied any low-flying birds that might be passing over the chimney stack. The back of his shirt was soaked in sweat: for a moment he had thought that Malcolm was going to rebel.

Hanbury began to say something about the need to support the private sector, but stopped when Dougal swung the Webley on him.

"I want you to stay quiet," Dougal said. He reinforced his desire by bringing down the butt of the Webley on Hanbury's kneecap. Hanbury squawked— as much in surprise as in pain. Malcolm looked shocked. Dougal bit back an urge to laugh.

"Right, Zelda," he said briskly, "why don't you get on with your story? We've got a rough idea why the CIA wants Vertag dead, and why you were chosen for the job. Take it from there."

"After I'd been briefed, I called James. He was happy to help—"

"I say," Hanbury interrupted, "*happy* isn't the word I would have chosen. You threatened to pass my curriculum vitae to one of your grubby little KGB chums. I could hardly refuse."

Zelda sighed. Her eyes remained on Dougal's face. "James needed a dramatic touch like that to make him feel important. But he had his own reasons to play ball: he's been getting worried about Vertag; he was glad to put the CIA in the position of owing him a favor; and he couldn't wait to help me with my expense account. As it's a dirty linen job, there's no risk of publicity. Your MI5 and Special Branch are strictly off limits for me. I can only use our London station facilities in the direct emergencies. James wanted to use you as a link man between me and Vertag to cover his ass still further. At the time, it seemed a good idea."

"What did he say about me?"

"That you needed money, you'd fit in with the Gravers and Vertag, you weren't on anyone's files, you could handle emergencies. . . . He implied he has some sort of a hold on you as well."

"Rubbish," Hanbury said. Dougal brought the revolver down on the other kneecap.

"He suggested I fly over to Rhodes to meet with you. I think the idea was that once the connection between you and me got on a personal level, he could have an even lower profile. It made sense to me too— I don't like operating blindly, and I wanted to check you out for myself. The timing seemed right, too— James needed some time to set things up with the Gravers. In my own mind, you were just part of a contingency plan we shouldn't have to use. James was going to tell me when Vertag was due, and I was going to be there in that ratty little wine bar when he walked in the door."

"Bang, bang, you're dead?"

Zelda nodded. "Something like that. But it didn't work out that way. For one thing Vertag got to England a day or so sooner than James had anticipated. He flew in last Thursday afternoon when I was halfway across the Atlantic. That Texas asshole at Langley wanted to bawl me out in person for not sending him Vertag's head in the diplomatic bag. Then there were other complications. Like on a personal level."

The last flame gleamed blue and died, leaving a blackened mound of melted polyethylene and paper ashes. Dougal attacked the smoking heap with the poker.

"Such as?" he asked.

"Well, I couldn't predict my metabolic reaction, could I, honey? I mean, I just didn't expect to get, uh, emotionally involved with an employee. That's the sort of thing they warn you against in basic training."

It felt as if Dougal's heart was executing a series of somersaults in his chest. He avoided Zelda's eyes and stared at the ashes in the fireplace.

"There was another complication, wasn't there?" His voice was cold and quiet. "You must have been able to calculate from what I told you on Friday night that I was resigning. You must have rung Hanbury, probably while I was out shopping in the morning. So you improvised a plan between you. James brought you here to meet Vertag, whenever he turned up. And he told the Gravers that he'd kidnapped you as a way of forcing me to stay in line. Am I right?"

207

"You got it." Zelda leaned forward as far as she could. "Honey, it was the best I could do. It got me and Vertag on collision course and cut out the need to involve you."

"Then why did you leave the message?"

"What message?"

"On the mirror in my flat. It said GRAVERS ELMNEY. Just enough information to let me find you."

"But I—" Zelda began.

"Ah," said Hanbury simultaneously. "I'm afraid that was my doing. It's really rather embarrassing. I assure you it had nothing to do with the photocopies you've just burned. My motive was altogether personal." He flashed a rueful smile at Dougal. "And sordid. I knew about the Gravers' safe, you see, and the money it contained. (Such a *silly* place to keep it.) But I don't know the combination. I intended to release you this evening and use your departure to suggest that you'd decamped with our hosts' movable assets into the bargain. I've already blackened your reputation with the Gravers by hinting you are a trifle light-fingered, along with all your other qualities. There would have been no danger to you, of course—I mean, the Gravers could hardly report the matter to the police, could they? As it is, you've rather neatly adapted my scheme for your own use. I don't hold it against you, William. All's fair in love and war."

"You," said Malcolm, with each word punctuated by the dull thud of the Colt's butt on Hanbury's head, "are the *pits*."

"No wonder we screwed up." Zelda glanced at Han-

208

bury. "If you ever work with me again, you cut out the private enterprise, okay?"

Hanbury squirmed on the sofa. "Yes, *ma'am*," he said in the sort of voice that belongs somewhere south of Atlanta.

"How did you screw it up this evening?" Malcolm asked.

Zelda shrugged. "James came down from his attic while I was waiting at the gatehouse. While he was immobilizing you two, Vertag arrived. I—well, I guess I panicked. I blew it by attacking too soon. I guess my Texan was right: my personality is basically inadequate when it comes to something as important as executive action. Vertag ran; I followed; William followed me. I had to knock him out for his own safety. But I lost Vertag. Shit, I lost myself. I'd still be sitting under a tree if James hadn't come to find me."

"So he's still out there?" Malcolm said. "He won't get far, not till it's properly light. It's not as if he knows the country."

Zelda shook her head sadly. "You don't know Vertag. He's in training for the end of the world. His idea of a vacation is to spend a couple of weeks in the Rockies with minimal equipment and no map. He's the sort of backpacker who doesn't need a backpack. A little stroll out there would be nothing to him. He's probably reached the other side of the country by now. He's too cute to hang around in your front yard. I guess I'll have to start looking for a new job."

The misery in Zelda's voice caught Dougal unawares; he could feel his sympathy wanting to reach out toward her. *Stop it, you sucker: it's probably all a bunch of lies.*

"And what," he asked harshly, "have you two seen fit to do with Fat Bert's body?"

CHAPTER 19

Lady Graver erupted from her tower aerie with a ferocity bred from despair and hampered by age. Her head sank into Malcolm's stomach. Malcolm sat down in the doorway, a look of astonishment on his face. Her foot slowly launched itself at his groin; he had ample time to avoid it.

"Bloody Nazis," she grunted, giving the second word its Churchillian pronunciation. She drew back her leg for another attempt.

Dougal hooked his right foot round her other ankle and clasped Lady Graver in the straitjacket of his arms. She felt like a large, skinny boiling fowl with a bad attack of delirium tremens. She struggled briefly, swore at length, and fell silent.

"We only came to let you go," Dougal said mildly. Malcolm got to his feet and dabbed ineffectually at the dust on his uniform trousers. Dougal relaxed his grip.

Lady Graver swayed against the wall. "There was

a time when I would have enjoyed that," she wheezed. "But not with you, hey?" Her finger jabbed Malcolm's chest. "I fancy Mr. Dougal is better equipped for wrestling with women."

"Will you be quiet, Lady Graver?" The words rumbled out of Dougal's mouth with whisky-precise dignity. "We're going to take you down to your friends and relations. After you've done a little job for us, we'll be on our way. Your favorite godson is here."

"You'll be free, you old bag," Malcolm said, straightening his tunic, "liberated from the lustful clutch of the thousand-year Reich."

"James? What's he doing here?"

"He never really left. After he brought Zelda to you, he cut back through the forest and hid in the attic. You can ask him why yourself."

"Well don't stand there dithering. Take me to him."

"Vertag turned up," he said conversationally as they reached the head of the stairs. "But he left in a hurry."

Lady Graver's grip tightened on his arm. "Thought I heard shouting. James—James always was a bit rash, you know."

"Ah." Dougal kept his voice noncommittal. Lady Graver seemed to put more weight on his arm. "Would you like a drink? I'm afraid we've raided your whiskies."

Lady Graver fastened both hands around Dougal's arm and launched herself onto the stairs. "If I don't have a drink soon," she said gruffly, "I'll bite someone's head off."

The lighting in this wing of the house was sparse.

Low-wattage bulbs, few and far between, emphasized the gloom. At Lady Graver's suggestion they avoided the courtyard and passed through the gatehouse, over the tunnel to the first floor of the main house. Just before they reached the library door, Lady Graver asked, "Where's Thomas? And Joe?"

"In the old nursery."

"And that black girl of yours?"

"She's not mine. She's with James in the library."

The door was ajar. Dougal kicked it open. Hanbury's head craned round toward them.

"Aunt Matilda. Thank God—I've been so worried about you. William, do give her a drink."

Dougal poured Lady Graver a good three fingers of Glenmorangie. As he turned to give it to her, he saw that the tears were still running down Zelda's cheeks.

Was the silent deluge caused by sorrow or by fear? It was difficult to credit a Company employee—if indeed she was—with becoming emotionally entangled with one of her victims. Perhaps she wept because Vertag was still alive. Not that it made much difference. Hanbury, Zelda, and the Gravers had treated Malcolm and himself as disposable pieces in a high-risk game.

"Ah, William, I wonder if you'd let us know what you mean to do with us?"

Hanbury's question was apparent in the eyes of Lady Graver and Zelda as well. The atmosphere in the room was heavy with a shared emotion that Dougal eventually defined as fear. He wasn't accustomed to other people being afraid.

"You're going to bury Fat Bert," he said suddenly.

213

"All of you. It's called accepting the consequences of your actions."

Bert's body, nailed in a packing case, had arrived in one of the Campernoyles vans the previous afternoon. The packing case had been deposited in the lee of the Range Rover in the garage. It was labeled "FRAGILE. THIS WAY UP," and it had been left upside down.

The interment took place in the northeast tower. The upper stories were ruined, but the undercroft had been roofed over with beams of untrimmed oak covered with strips of corrugated iron. The space beneath was used as a garden shed.

It was some time before the burial party was mustered and ready to dig. Sir Thomas and Joe were stiff and numb and needed time to get their circulation going. Lady Graver used the breathing space to consume at least a pair of hands' worth of whisky. By the time they reached the courtyard, she was humming Fats Waller numbers and beating time on Hanbury's arm.

It was she who had chosen the site of the grave: it was a secluded spot; the ground had been thoroughly turned over during the most recent excavation at Elmney, so there was little risk that future archaeologists would disturb Fat Bert; and, since the earth had been dug so recently, it should be relatively easy to shift.

The workers began by clearing a space among the contents of the shed. Lady Graver held the torch aloft and provided a running commentary.

"Good God, I haven't seen those shears since Johnnie died. . . . It's about time we got rid of those seed boxes.

Look, Thomas, they're wormy. Put them on one side for the bonfire. . . . Woodlice! I can't abide woodlice. Stamp on them, James, quickly."

Malcolm escorted Joe and Hanbury to collect the body. They carried the packing case with difficulty; Hanbury complained bitterly about a splinter. They wrenched it open and found Bert in the fetal position, with his head set at an angle to his torso that it had never achieved in life. Death had deflated his body. It stank abominably. Hanbury propped him up against the wall and wiped his fingers fastidiously on his handkerchief.

"Do we really need this, ah, *memento mori* while we dig? If we covered him up, he wouldn't cast such a blight on the proceedings."

"But that's the idea, James," said Dougal dryly. He could hear the two male Gravers retching painfully in the courtyard. Lady Graver looked up at the ceiling. Her humming modulated from 'Two Sleepy People' to something that sounded suspiciously like the Kyrie from Fauré's Requiem.

Zelda walked as if in a dream toward Fat Bert and gently closed his eyes.

Dougal cleared his throat. "Come on, get digging."

The storm lantern on one side of the shed and Lady Graver's torch on the other threw the shadows of the four gravediggers on the rounded surface of the whitewashed walls. Hanbury with the pickax was breaking the ground; Zelda and Joe were spading it out, while Sir Thomas shoveled the loose earth into a crumbling rampart around the deepening depression in the center of the shed.

Malcolm and Dougal were on either side of the doorway with a bottle strategically sited between them. Neither of them took their eyes from their captives; it would be foolish to allow a workers' revolution to break out.

"Why are we bothering to stay?" Malcolm asked quietly.

Dougal shrugged. "Call it poetic justice. I want to see them tidy up part of the mess they've made. Besides it'll be safer for us in the long run if no loose ends are left. Imagine what would have happened if the char or someone had walked in to find five people tied up and one corpse on the premises. I just want to get it all *over.*"

Malcolm glanced quickly at him. "You've caught a bad dose of the morals, haven't you? But you're right. This way they're all implicated. . . . Wow!"

Joe had removed his shirt. The lamplight gleamed on his damp skin, giving his complexion a warmth it lacked in daylight.

"Not bad, eh? He strips better than you'd think."

"I don't think about it at all," said Dougal. "You're not planning to see him again, are you?"

"Might drop into Campernoyles at some point. *He*'d like me to. You can always tell. He enjoyed me tying him up."

"He won't want to see you after tonight. Quite apart from anything else, you pinched his family fortune out of the safe. And he'll probably blame you for the disappearance of his heroin."

"I say, how much farther do you want us to go?"

216

Hanbury's head and shoulders, stained with earth and sweat, reared out of the hole. "Surely three feet down will be enough."

"Okay." Dougal hardened himself and said to Zelda, "You'd better go through Bert's pockets. Check round his neck too."

Zelda silently obeyed. She handled Bert as if he were alive, as if she were a nurse and he her patient. She brought her meager haul to Dougal: a few pounds in notes, some medically prescribed Librium, and a stained handkerchief with frayed corners. Hanbury and Joe swung the body into its grave.

Dougal gave the signal and the soil rained into the grave. At least Bert was waiting all in one piece for the second coming.

The earth displaced would not fit back in the hole. Dougal made them stamp it down. The remainder was scattered in the garden. He was unprepared for the effect that finishing the job had. Graver, Joe, and Hanbury solemnly shook hands. They had the look of men who had completed an arduous but worthwhile task; physical labor could be its own justification.

Lady Graver flashed the torch across the floor. "Concrete," she said triumphantly. "You boys can do it tomorrow. It'll keep the place much drier. I wonder why I didn't think of it before. But now we all deserve a drink and perhaps something to eat. Come along."

At that point the evening—or rather the morning—shifted a few degrees from the course Dougal had expected. He had envisaged that he and Malcolm would beat a rapid retreat—and that none of the seven people at present in the castle would have anything to say to each other.

His reckoning had failed to take into account the effects of physical tiredness, emotional relief, alcohol, and the late flowering of Lady Graver's instincts as a hostess.

There was whisky, followed by more whisky, followed by an early breakfast of eggs, bacon, and mushrooms cooked and served by Joe and Malcolm. The party returned from the kitchen to the library for coffee and more alcohol.

To Dougal it seemed that the evening had been taken over by a film director with a strong attachment to surrealism. At some point he played backgammon with Lady Graver for anatomical stakes; he lost a leg, an arm, and three ribs. Hanbury took over his place at the board, won them back from Lady Graver, and presented them to Dougal. "Please," he said, "as a small token of my esteem."

Sir Thomas cornered Dougal by the fireplace and told him about one of his putative ancestors once more. Dougal listened politely. They had just buried a corpse: now they were burying its memory with a wake. He wondered where Vertag was. He didn't share the others' unstated assumption that the American had disappeared from their lives forever. Vengeance, security, and greed supplied three counterarguments. Vertag might accept that he had lost a battle, but that would only increase his determination to win the war.

Malcolm and Joe talked intensely in the window seat. Dougal was called across to receive a financial proposition. Malcolm claimed to believe that Elmney Castle had great potential for conversion to a luxury hotel. Joe would provide culinary expertise; the other Gravers would circulate among the guests, behaving in a picturesque and suitably aristocratic fashion; while Malcolm would supply, with a little help from Dougal, a slice of capital and the requisite managerial skills.

Dougal declined—not so much because of the idea's commercial viability but because he felt a pressing need to get rid of his breakfast.

When he returned, purged but not chastened, he ran into James Hanbury.

"You see?" Hanbury said, throwing his arms wide, "everything's fine. Trust your Uncle James."

"That's the last thing I'd do." Dougal crossed to the sofa and sat down beside Zelda, who was nursing a bottle of Glenfiddich as if it were the last bottle of whisky in existence. Dougal gently pulled it from her arms and poured some of its contents into her glass.

"Aw, honey," she said, "I thought you'd never come and talk to me."

"I've come to say goodbye." The alcohol had contrived to cancel itself out. He felt lucid, though light-headed—so light that the smallest untoward movement seemed capable of tumbling his mind out of his body.

"I'm sorry." Zelda leaned forward, presenting Dougal with a view that momentarily distracted him from her words. "I've never had my job in conflict with my private life before. I guess I didn't handle it very well. I was really happy that night in your apartment."

Dougal, presented with the opportunity to hurt with a lie, told the truth: "So was I." He took her left hand on impulse. The digging had raised pink blisters on the palm. "Look on the bright side," he began, but could find no way to go on. The hand was warm, with long delicate fingers. Dougal hurriedly dropped it and stood up.

"We must be going," he mumbled, like a guest going through the motions of farewell at a dinner party with his mind already on the long drive home. "Malcolm!"

Malcolm looked up. He and Joe were now sharing a joint, but Dougal noticed that the Colt was still weighing down one side of Malcolm's tunic.

"I suppose we'd better," he said. He passed the joint to Joe. "I'll ring you at Campernoyles in a couple of days, okay?"

"Right." Joe looked owlishly at the man who had broken his glasses. "We can hammer out a conversion of premises proposal. We'll have to form a company, of course."

"I don't see any problem there." Malcolm added gravely, "In principle, at least. I'm a little uncertain about some of the practical details—like the fallout shelter under the gatehouse, for instance."

"You're not going?" Lady Graver said. "Why not stay for a few days? Plenty of beds, you know."

"We must be off," Dougal said firmly. He could feel the Volvo's keys in his pocket. "If you don't mind, we might borrow one of your cars. We'll leave it with Joe in London."

"Of course," said Lady Graver with a majestic wave of her arm. "One cannot do without a motor these days."

"You'll be at the flat?" Hanbury asked. "I'll telephone you when I get back to town. We could have dinner together."

"I think I'll be going away very soon." Dougal turned away. "Come on, Malcolm. It'll be dawn soon."

Malcolm picked up the suitcase. Dougal was relieved to see that Hanbury was the only one who noticed the action: he gave a nod of approval, but said nothing. The whole party trailed down to the hall after Dougal and Malcolm, still apparently under the illusion that favored guests were departing.

"You drive," Malcolm said to Dougal as they reached the courtyard. He stopped suddenly and hit his forehead theatrically. "Blow! Must spend a penny." He darted back into the hall before anyone had time to react.

Dougal got the car started while the male Gravers and Hanbury swung open the double gates. Suddenly Zelda and her luggage materialized beside his open window.

"Can you give me a ride? I think I'll go crazy if I stay here."

Dougal's mouth went dry. He turned and unlocked the rear door. At the same moment, Malcolm appeared on the passenger side. He flung himself in at the same moment as Zelda collapsed on the back seat. Malcolm jerked the Colt between her and Dougal. "You're mad." The pronoun might have been singular or plural.

Zelda made a noise without words in the back of the car. Dougal put the car into gear and edged toward the tunnel of the gatehouse.

"Zelda! What are you doing?" Hanbury was beside the car, rapping frantically on the window. There was a click as Zelda engaged the door lock. "We have business to discuss—"

Dougal waved and put his foot down on the accelerator. The car hurtled into the narrow tunnel. There was a screech of metal as the side of the car rubbed against the gate post. Dougal shifted into second gear and sent the car roaring down the drive.

"Feeling better?" Malcolm leaned over to push in the choke.

Dougal wondered if he was imagining the sound of Hanbury's voice through the open window: "Business . . . important business . . ."

"Yes," he said. "A lot better."

CHAPTER 20

Dougal's driving became less tempestuous once he reached third gear. By the time he reached top, it could almost be called tranquil. Malcolm stopped holding on to his seat belt.

"Go to that forest car park. We'll change into the van. Mind that sheep, for God's sake."

Dougal silently obeyed. He brought the car to a halt, with a jerk that sent the gravel skidding.

"Neat, eh?" Malcolm said smugly. "I pulled the telephone wires out when I pretended to go to the loo. There's not a working vehicle left in the castle. Once we're in the van, they'll have no way of tracing us."

"Not neat," said Dougal, more for the pleasure of contradiction than for any other reason. "Hanbury must have hidden his car somewhere; it's probably parked in the forest."

"What about her?" Malcolm gestured with his thumb toward the back of the car. "We could rip the leads out of this car and leave her here. Safer all round you know. Auntie Sam's quite capable of dishing out karate chops from the back seat. Sam as in Little Black Sambo."

"That's enough," Dougal rapped. (*Good God, I sound just like my father.*) He had in fact been considering leaving Zelda with the Volvo, but Malcolm's phrasing had killed the attraction of the idea. He had had enough of pretending to be brutal.

"You do what you want, honey," Zelda said quietly. "I need a little breathing space, and I guess you do too. But I appreciate you probably won't want to spend it together."

Malcolm's lips vibrated with a large raspberry.

Dougal switched on the interior light of the car. "Pass me that suitcase, would you?"

Zelda heaved it over the seats. Dougal snapped back the catches and extracted a wad of notes. He closed the case and pushed it across to Malcolm.

"You can take that and the van to London," he said curtly. "You'd better change your clothes in case you're stopped by a real copper. Don't go to the flat—Hanbury might want a share of the money and that's the first place he'd look. But get in touch with Nick and I'll contact you through him. We can divide the cash in a day or two."

"I hope you know what you're doing."

"You said that before, remember?" Dougal jabbed a finger toward the suitcase. "At least knight errantry proved to be profitable. Just let me make my own mistakes."

Malcolm said nothing. Dougal knew he was acting ungraciously; responsibility and violence had left him depressed, and he was taking it out on a friend who deserved better. *If only Malcolm wasn't so damned jolly about it.*

"I'm sorry." Dougal touched Malcolm's shoulder. "It's just that I don't enjoy this sort of thing and you do. It grates. Give me a day or two and I'll feel human again."

"Okay." Malcolm opened his door and slid his legs outside. He looked back. "I still think you should leave that woman here. Or is she part of being human?"

"I don't know," Dougal said, trying to ignore the misery that suddenly welled up within him. "I just don't know."

The two vehicles soon parted company. Malcolm went south toward Chepstow, the M4, and the Severn Bridge; motorway breakfasts had a morbid attraction for him. Dougal and Zelda drove through the forest in the direction of the A48 and Gloucester.

The Volvo seemed to have a will of its own and a positive dislike for its driver. It thundered round bends like a bolting horse and had a tendency to drift off the road when Dougal's mind was elsewhere. He eventually cut his speed to a sedate thirty miles per hour.

Through the windshield, the world rushed toward him. The infinite green of the forest looked as if it had just emerged from a superior dry cleaners, a perfect complement to the early morning blue of the sky. Scraps of cloud bearing a strong resemblance to pink meringues were escaping toward the horizon. The road bucked, turned, climbed, and fell, tracing the contours of the land like a lover. The car crested a hill and swung east; the sun was emerging from the distant haze of the Cotswolds. Dougal squinted through fire-tipped lashes and swerved to avoid the splintered corpse of a hedgehog. The Severn, transmuted into a river of copper, flashed a warning.

"Clear as the sun," Zelda muttered unexpectedly, just on the edge of Dougal's hearing. *"And terrible as an army with banners."*

A savage joy that he was still alive pierced Dougal. As the pain ebbed, he remembered the clockwork train set he had been given on his fourth birthday: *It can't be mine. There must be a mistake. Someone will take it away.*

All he wanted was a little certainty and a time for convalescence. Zelda could supply the certainty, a quality that had been conspicuously absent from the last few days. It all came down to the reason why she wanted to accompany him.

She might want to kill him, as an inconvenient witness to a sordid little CIA failure. Alternatively, she might have told the truth in the library: even a CIA hitwoman could fall in love.

The Webley was tucked between Dougal's right leg and the car seat. Zelda was now beside him in the front of the car.

Dougal sighed. There was really only one way to find out. If he was wrong, at least Malcolm was out of harm's way.

Gloucester came into view, with the gray cathedral tower sprouting from its midst. Dougal negotiated a curve in a manner that caused the lorry behind him to flash its lights hysterically.

He reached for the Webley with his left hand, picking it up by the barrel. "Here," he said, keeping his eyes on the road, "would you shove that in the glove compartment?"

"Sure. . . . William, why don't we dump this car? I don't want to be negative about your driving, but we could relax much more on a train or a bus."

The first London-bound train of the day left Gloucester at 6:30 A.M. It was not in fact going to London, but to Swindon, where they would have to change for Paddington.

Dougal and Zelda waited on the platform. A group of laborers, armed with cigarettes, were discussing page three of the *Sun* in exhaustive anatomical detail. There were three older men in suits, clutching briefcases like shields and wrapped in the trance of an unpleasant but familiar early morning routine. An older couple, flanked by heavily labeled suitcases, were checking through a capacious carryall with an intensity that suggested their survival would later depend on its contents. A man of Dougal's age in a rumpled leather jacket was frowning at a paperback copy of the poems of Villon; it was difficult to decide whether he was disgusted with his reading matter or with himself for choosing it at this time of the day.

Zelda whispered, "No problem here. We look like people on vacation. Why you smiling, honey?"

"Because we left the whole of last weekend behind with that car in the station car park. Besides, I like wearing your jersey."

This was true. Zelda, noticing the crop of goose pimples on Dougal's arms, had insisted on clothing him. The jersey smelled of her: clean, with a tang to add

227

flavor. The loan was an oddly reassuring gesture that dissolved, irrationally but completely, the vestiges of Dougal's doubts about Zelda. If she wanted to kill him, she would not have lent him her sky blue jersey with the line of purple penguins on front. It was as simple as that.

"Nothing will take away this weekend." Zelda stared bleakly at the deserted platform opposite them. "I never thought executive action was like this. Scary, yes. But not so damn stupid."

"Stupid?"

"I don't mean I shouldn't have tried. It's better that Vertag should die. I accepted the possibility of things like that when I took the job. Someone has to do the dirty work. If the CIA didn't exist, we'd have to invent it. Up to now, I was lucky. I could keep my hands clean. But I can't complain now they're dirty. I can't run away from the dirt."

It was a plea. Dougal said gently, "It's like hygiene on a big scale. I suppose you must never forget why you need to get rid of the dirt. Bleach can be as harmful as shit. And as useful."

His tone was soothing; but the words were too ambiguous to be comforting. Zelda put a hand on his arm but continued to stare away.

"It was stupid because it failed." She swallowed. "Because of the mess. Because of the way other people's motives got tangled with mine." The hand burrowed deeper into the warmth between Dougal's arm and body. "Because of you."

Dougal brought his free hand round to cover hers.

228

Zelda turned her head at last. She was standing so close that their cheeks grazed one another. He could hear her breathing, fast and shallow, and feel her lashes rasping soundlessly over his stubble. He regretted for an instant that he hadn't thought to shave before leaving Elmney. His lips were beginning to twist into a smile when Zelda killed both regret and amusement with her next words.

"I can't stop now. You understand that, baby? It's not just that I'm an organization woman and the Company will fire me if I fail. If I walk away and wash my hands, I'll never get them clean again. I still need to believe in *me.*"

They walked along the platform in an unspoken agreement to put more distance between themselves and the other passengers. On the left their single, lumpen shadow slithered silently beside them.

"I couldn't have said that," Dougal said, grasping at the nearest generality to take his mind from an entirely particular despair. "The English tend to think that straightforward statements of personal ideals are invasions of privacy. Or rather sinful continental luxuries, like bidets in the bathroom. Americans are much saner in that respect."

Saner? He thought of Vertag with his Nuremberg rally for one in Campernoyles.

"Vertag." Zelda plucked the name from Dougal's mind. "He'll have headed for the nearest city. Maybe he's hitching. If I were him, I guess I'd make for London. The airports there give him more flexibility than a provincial one. And he's probably got resources there too. I'm gonna have to get the London station head to give me some manpower. Old redneck will blow a blood vessel when he hears."

"You've only got a very slim chance," said Dougal, pretending he was a columnist dealing with an anonymous problem. "Is it worth it? You'll certainly upset the people at Langley still more. It would just give Vertag forewarning of your intentions, if his intelligence is as good as they claim. And what if the manhunt is leaked to the press? Questions in Parliament. Our government won't like it; nor will yours. Are you sure—?"

"Honey," Zelda snarled, an incongruous sound from an ebony Venus with tears glistening like snail tracks on her face, "you stop treating me like the little woman, okay? I know the score and I can add it up on my own. I wish you'd stop talking and kiss me."

The kiss lasted until their train was announced. Three small, shabby carriages crawled toward them, dwarfed even more by what was reputedly the longest platform in England. The train jerked to a halt and brought the waiting passengers back to life. Most people went in the front carriage; the laborers chose the center one, the smoker; Dougal and Zelda climbed aboard the last.

Apart from themselves, it contained only one other traveler—the student of Villon, who positioned himself as far away as possible, near the narrow door that led to the rest of the train. Zelda stared around her in amazement.

"Gee, you Brits sure know how to travel in style."

She ran her fingernail over the faded surface of the gray upholstery, raising a thin whorl of dust, which turned gold in the sunshine. She found a hole, clearly the work of a passenger with time and a knife on his hands. Her finger explored the irregular slashes. Dougal silently watched as the jagged NF symbol of the National Front emerged. Probably another of Vertag's patrons, at some remove. Zelda prodded the stuffing beneath: "Dream home for mobile bedbugs, huh?"

"Zelda." The desperation in Dougal's voice almost made their fellow passenger turn round; there was a perceptible, though immediately disciplined twitch of the head. He lowered his voice. "Once we reach London, I won't help you find Vertag. It's not just that I'm scared. And it's not that I don't want to see you."

The guard's whistle sounded shrilly immediately outside their open window. A door slammed. The train shuddered as it tried to whip up some enthusiasm for the journey. There was movement on the platform: someone running for the train.

"Love the sinner, hate the sin?" Zelda poked the bundle of notes in the pocket of Dougal's shirt. "Different sins but maybe the same love. Or whatever you call it."

The train had just begun to move. Dougal was remotely aware of a door opening and shutting in the middle of their carriage, and of a sigh of relief. The late passenger had just made it in time. Suddenly Zelda enveloped him with her body. They fell sideways along their seat. Pleasure rapidly succeeded surprise in Dougal's mind. It was, after all, the first time that he had

231

had Zelda comprehensively within his grasp. His lips searched for hers, but her mouth was jammed against his ear.

"Keep *down*," she hissed. "It's Vertag."

It was all of a piece with the NF symbol, at least in the dreamlike state of confusion that replaced Dougal's pleasure. Vertag needed transport and it was perfectly reasonable that he should find the nearest station on the Intercity network. And it was only to be expected that, in a universe where chance was only one law among many, the three of them should find themselves in the same carriage. Vertag knew that he was in no immediate danger from the police and that his enemies were unable to monitor the public transport system with any efficiency. He didn't know that Zelda was from the CIA. He didn't even know what—

"He's never seen me," Zelda whispered. "I was in the dark the whole time. But he knows you, so for God's sake keep below the seat back."

"Does he know your voice?"

"Uh-huh. It wasn't one of those interpersonally articulate meetings. But—"

A door clicked and Zelda buried Dougal's face in the haven of her breasts. There were heavy footsteps in the carriage.

"If you can spare a moment," said a slow, Gloucestershire voice above them, "I need to see your tickets."

Dougal felt himself flushing. Zelda pulled their tickets from his pocket and handed them to the guard with a smile. The guard clipped the tickets and handed them back. His brown, lined face remained impassive. His faded eyes peered shortsightedly at them; they were half hidden by a thick and unruly crop of white hair. The British Rail cap that perched insecurely on top made him look like an Old English sheepdog taking part, unwillingly but with perfect good manners, in a TV commercial for the Age of the Train.

Dougal peered back, though with more interest. But surely even Hanbury couldn't have managed to pull off this particular disguise in the time available?

The guard bent confidentially toward them. "You'll be all right till Stonehouse, or even Stroud, I shouldn't wonder. That's when it'll begin to fill up."

They remained entwined as the guard examined the tickets of the other two passengers.

"How long will he be gone?" Zelda whispered. As she spoke, the train, tired out by its exertions, reduced its speed to a crawl.

"Maybe a minute or two. If he's a mate of the driver, he might stay at the front of the train for a while."

Zelda was on her feet before he had finished the sentence. She walked unhesitatingly to the lavatory cubicle at the end of the train. Dougal could hear her pumping the handle on the door with increasing vehemence. She returned along the gangway, briefly touching Dougal's shoulder with a gesture that meant more than that he should keep his head low. Dougal touched wood in much the same spirit. Only his head was available, but he had always found it an acceptable substitute for the real thing.

The train ground to a halt. Zelda needed all the luck he could give her. She was acting as rashly as a gambler in pursuit of a winning streak. Vertag was a street-fighter whose defensive instincts must be screwed up to their highest pitch. He must have seen or heard that the black woman approaching him was not alone. The guard could return, or the student might decide his eyes needed a rest from the tortuous mind of a fifteenth-century Parisian hoodlum.

"Pardon me," he heard her saying. Then, in a lower voice, as if she was bending closer, "I can't open the bathroom door. My friend's about to throw up. I gotta get him in there quick."

"Sure, don't you worry." Vertag's nasal voice was as incisive as ever but sounded unexpectedly warm. Perhaps he, like Dougal, responded to maidens in distress with atypical altruism. Dougal gave a low moan whose realism owed as much to necessity as to guile.

They moved down the aisle, with Zelda in the lead. Dougal pressed his head against the seat and tried to conceal the rest of his face with his arm. He still had a clear, though limited field of vision.

Zelda bent down to pat his forehead as she passed. He noticed she had undone another button of her shirt: she was relying on other factors than luck in her pursuit of the winning streak.

Vertag crowded behind her. He was wearing muddy jeans and a green sweatshirt with a ripped collar. A gold chain glinted around his neck. His dark hair was ruffled, and a long, recent scratch ran diagonally across his cheek. He looked more than ever like a gypsy— the sort of gypsy who could seduce your daughter, steal your silver, and persuade you to buy a gross of clothespegs to match your tumble dryer.

"Hi," he said. "Too much of that tepid beer?"

The eyes remained the same, and the voice was still

warm, but a prong of stainless steel had somehow sprouted from Vertag's hand. It twinkled like tinsel in the sunlight. Zelda had half turned away, her body poised for the last few yards to the lavatory. The knife blade began to describe a gentle arc that would deposit its point in Zelda's rib cage. From there it would glide on to prick the life out of her heart. It was like a television killing, slowed down on the video so one could appreciate the finer details of the logistics involved.

Dougal was next aware that the video machine had been thrust into its fast-forward mode. His feet dug back at the side to the carriage, to give him impetus; his left arm hammered down on the seat for elevation. He bucked forward and locked his hand round Vertag's hairy, sinewy wrist.

A hand chopped across at him. It bruised his shoulder but might well have snapped his collarbone if the struggling of Vertag's other arm had not tugged Dougal a few inches to the right. As it was, the pain numbed him. He knew that his grip on Vertag's wrist would be broken at any moment.

Dougal lunged with his last available weapon: his head. His jaws snapped round Vertag's index finger. His teeth sunk through skin, flesh, and gristle and jarred against bone.

The blade—an elegant, bone-handled flick-knife—slithered through Vertag's brown fingers. It landed point downward on the floor of the carriage, where it stuck for an instant before keeling over.

Vertag pivoted, allowing Dougal to get his other hand round the wrist. He tried to turn it. A drop of blood oozed from the mangled finger and became a red star on the toe of one of Vertag's white sneakers.

Why hasn't Vertag screamed?

His eyes slid up the American's writhing body to find the answer. Vertag's mouth was buried in the crook of Zelda's elbow.

As Dougal watched, she sliced the edge of her free hand against Vertag's neck. He wondered if he imagined a dry snap. The muscles of Vertag's body became limp. Zelda's casual efficiency reminded Dougal of the way an angler kills a fish.

He glanced down the carriage. The door at the end was still closed. All that could be seen of the fourth passenger was the back of a dark head bent over its book.

Zelda abruptly let go of Vertag. The body crumpled into Dougal's arms. He was aware that Zelda was stumbling toward the lavatory. He glanced up as the door closed. There was a click as the bolt shot home. The sign on the door said ENGAGED.

Dougal lowered Vertag on to the seat, retrieved the knife, and scuffed a fleck of blood into the grime of the floor. The passenger in the front of the carriage still hadn't moved. Perhaps he had interpreted the muted sounds of the struggle as the evidence of illness. There was a lot to be said for British reticence.

The entrails of the train grumbled beneath Dougal's feet, reminding him that something had to be done about the corpse, which slouched inelegantly in the seat behind him. They couldn't leave Vertag where he was: the train would be filling up, and the dead had no inhibitions about revealing their condition to the living.

236

Afterward the memory of what he now did astonished him when awake and haunted him when asleep. His actions were swift, efficient, and strangely unimpeded by fear. He was aware of the consequences of failure but was briefly undisturbed by them: it was as if matchsticks had replaced bank notes in the middle of a game of poker.

The train was stranded on an embankment, surrounded by the unlovely southern fringes of Gloucester. On the near side, a few feet from the carriage, the ground sloped sharply down to a broad ditch that was crammed with a mass of uncultivated greenery—hawthorn, elder, rosebay willow herb, foxglove, hedge parsley, and the largest nettles Dougal had ever seen. A tall wooden fence prevented this elongated wilderness from contaminating the trim allotments that lay beyond. Not ideal: but there was no guarantee that a better opportunity would present itself before the guard returned or the train reached Stonehouse.

The train shuddered, nudged six inches farther down the line, and subsided with a wheeze. Dougal's hands frantically searched for Vertag's possessions. There was nothing in the jeans, but a canvas money belt beneath the loose folds of the sweatshirt repaid his efforts. He stuffed the two passports, one Canadian, one Swiss, and neither of them in the name of Vertag, into Zelda's holdall, together with an airline ticket to Rome and an International Driver's Licence. The neatly arranged wad of large-denomination bills in assorted currencies went into his own back pocket. Finally, Dougal ripped the gold chain from Vertag's neck. A thin disc was attached to it: one side was blank, while the other was engraved with the number 666. That went into Zelda's bag as well. No doubt it would please the bureaucrats at Langley to know the precise identity of their victim.

With a quick glance toward the front of the carriage, Dougal seized Vertag's arms, turned and hauled the body onto his shoulders in a graceless parody of the fireman's lift. The train began to move as he did so, nearly jerking him off his feet. He shuffled beneath his burden to the nearest door.

The door opened easily. Dougal let it swing back against the side of the carriage; he was grateful that the train hadn't yet picked up speed. He took a deep breath and heaved the body away from him with such singleminded enthusiasm that he nearly followed it himself.

Vertag toppled slowly down the embankment. The acceleration of the train made it seem that he was shrinking as he fell. In seconds he was no more than a loose-limbed cuddly toy lying discarded and concealed among the nettles. Dougal watched a diminishing speck of white among the green: at this distance Vertag's sneaker could well be hedge parsley.

"Excuse me."

Dougal swung away from the open doorway. The saturnine face of his fellow passenger was frowning at him. The man was on his feet and moving down the aisle. Dougal dropped his eyes from that accusing gaze and found himself staring at the cover of the Villon in the man's hand: it showed two men hanging from a gibbet. His mind was racing as uselessly as an engine revving in neutral. He noticed dully that Vertag's knife had found its way into the palm of his

238

own hand; his thumb massaged the button that released the blade.

The stranger was saying something, but the meaning of his words was chasing down the rails after Vertag's sneaker. The knife grew hot and heavy in Dougal's hand. There was a buzzing in his ears that was trying to drown the sound of the stranger's voice.

The bolt on the lavatory door shot back with a crack like that of a small-bore rifle. Zelda, unsmiling but steady, stood on the threshold. The buzzing abruptly stopped. Dougal slid the knife back into his pocket.

". . . I wondered if I could help you close the door," their fellow passenger was saying. His voice was unexpectedly soft and hesitant. "Are you all right?"

"Yes. I felt a bit sick a moment ago and leaned out of the window for some air. The door can't have been latched properly." Dougal rubbed his aching eyes. "I nearly fell out."

"Let me." The stranger extended a long arm and pulled the door back into its frame. He smiled at Dougal with the embarrassment of a well-brought-up Good Samaritan, nodded awkwardly in Zelda's direction, and scuttled back to the security of his seat.

"Thanks," Dougal said quietly. He turned to Zelda and closed her hand around Vertag's knife. "We'd better leave the train at Swindon. Then we go our separate ways. Understand?"

He lacked the courage to wait for a reply. He fled, without looking back, to the malodorous seclusion of the lavatory.

CHAPTER 21

Zelda's nipples reared from her substantial breasts like twin towers of Saint Michael on a pair of Glastonbury Tors. Dougal's tongue climbed each Tor and tower by the scenic route—two matching spirals that led to rose-red summits. Having conquered these peaks, Dougal descended to the valley between them and wondered whether to move north or south.

"I guess we should put some clothes on, sweetheart."

North, Dougal decided. He traveled up to Zelda's mouth and briefly prevented it from making another suggestion. A minute later they rolled apart.

Zelda stretched. They had lost the covers some time ago and her long black body was outlined against the white sheet. The sight sent Dougal's hand down to the lowlands south of the Glastonbury Tors. Zelda captured his hand in both of hers.

"I'm going to take a shower," she said.

"I'll keep you company."

"No way, William. You know what happened last time. We're late already."

Dougal lay back as she padded from the bed to the bathroom. She left the door open. They had recuperated together for three days; his decision to leave her at Swindon had been easy to make but impossible to put into effect. Now, Dougal realized unwillingly, the convalescence was nearly over. The outside world, like cheerfulness, was always breaking in.

His eyes moved round the comfortable disorder of their hotel bedroom. The litter of their occupation had long since destroyed its anonymity. The management's oatmeal carpet was upstaged by the chaotic colors of a large Turkish kilim. Zelda had bought it for him from a New Bond Street carpet shop where the sales staff had the knack of looking down at you, even when you were taller. She had used—as for every major purchase of the last few days—her American Express card, confident in her belief that the CIA would consider the pampering of William Dougal a legitimate expense. Dougal himself suspected that in the long run the CIA might not be as generous as Zelda. In one important sense it did not really matter who paid for Dougal's little luxuries at the end of the line. It was the present that counted. Zelda needed to propitiate some dark gods of her own; and one of her chosen methods of expiation was to pay for everything.

Dougal stared unseeingly at the books, papers, and clothes that partially obscured the kilim. He hoped her rituals were taking effect at last. On Monday and Tuesday nights she woke Dougal with cries like a hunted animal's, shivering in her sleep and gleaming eerily with sweat. Last night, however, she had slept serenely.

His own memories of the last few days might have belonged to someone else. It was a humiliating tribute to the power of nicotine: the struggle between will and craving turned the rest of life into a side issue.

At least the tobacco war was now on the wane. Apart from scattered skirmishes, the conflict had settled down to the stylized, routine confrontations of a cold war. Willpower would have lost if there had been a cigarette machine aboard the 6:30 to Swindon, when a tobacco-nourished fatalism appeared to be the one philosophy for a rational person.

The familiar desire stirred like a serpent within him. He rolled off the bed and sat in front of the dressing table. He picked up a boxed bar of soap and offered it to his reflection.

"Cigarette?"

His reflection dropped the box and gave a dismissive wave. "No thanks. I don't smoke."

Zelda emerged from the bathroom, toweling herself vigorously. "You tell him, baby."

Dougal sighed. He watched the lips of his reflection move. "I just hope he's listening."

They took a taxi to the airport. At first both of them were able to ignore where they were going. But once they were past Hammersmith and on the M4, their conversation died. It was replaced by disconnected remarks that already had a private Atlantic between them.

"I'll call you at Nick's. . . . Don't call my apartment,

those jerks have probably put a tap on my phone."

"I could come over in the autumn maybe. Once they've finished debriefing you."

"You remember the post restante arrangements for letters? I'm Dora Humbleton."

"You might miss the flight."

"I hope not. They're already going to have my ass for taking three days off."

"You can see Windsor Castle from the M4. But we won't—it comes after Heathrow."

"Everything's so small in this country. Even the freeways."

"We're going to be late."

They reached the terminal after Zelda's flight had been called. There was no time for farewells, a mercy for which they both were grateful.

Zelda checked in and was shooed into the departure lounge by the airline staff. She kissed Dougal.

"Aw, hell, honey," she said over her shoulder, "why do you always make me cry?"

Dougal picked his way through the bright subterranean labyrinth to the underground platform. A train was waiting. He sat in a nonsmoking carriage and watched as distraught travelers piled themselves and their luggage on board.

A train was better than a taxi. You didn't have to decide where you wanted to go beforehand. In his present mood Dougal thought he might stay in his seat until the end of the line, which in this case was the absurdly named Cockfosters.

Only thirty-five stops to go to one of the silliest names in the world!

He must have spoken the words aloud. Three Japanese businessmen were pretending not to look at him. Two pink British parents were shepherding their even pinker family to the other end of the carriage. Probably his fly was undone too. Perhaps his peeling suntan looked like one of the symptoms of leprosy. He wished he was eight miles high over the Atlantic.

The train rushed toward Hatton Cross and the three Hounslows. Cool, stale air rushed through the carriage as someone came through from the neighboring smoker. The air brought a hint of tobacco, a scent from a lost paradise.

Dougal continued to stare at the ribbed floor of the carriage. A white cigarette butt landed a few inches away from his foot. An elegant brown shoe descended on it and gave a vicious twist.

"May I join you?" asked James Hanbury.

"By all means."

Hanbury sat down beside Dougal and stared hard at an advertisement opposite. It warned how bad breath could affect your social life and proposed an expensive solution.

"Awkward," he said at last. "I'd hoped to have a word with Zelda before she went. Just missed her. I only found out which hotel you were in this morning. You could have had a lift to Heathrow in my taxi."

"Maybe Zelda and I preferred to go it alone."

"I'm sure you could pass a message on. In any case, I'm glad to have a word with you on your own. We freelance operatives are at such a disadvantage, eh? It cost me a small fortune to find out which flight Zelda would be on, and then the traffic made me late."

Dougal stared at his hands and wondered if they were strong enough to strangle someone.

"We need one another, William. Now more than ever. We're threatened by the same Scylla and Charybdis. Alex and his backers aren't the sort who forgive and forget. And Zelda's employers aren't going to turn a blind eye to our involvement. You must appreciate the gravity of the situation: an American subject attacked by an agent of the very organization that's supposed to protect Americans. It's political dynamite, dear boy. Watergate would look like a playground squabble in comparison."

The train was slowing. Hanbury was speeding up.

"They can keep Zelda quiet, of course. But what about us? We're a couple of extremely inconvenient foreign nationals as far as they're concerned. It's a pound to a penny that they'll put out a contract on us. Unless we coordinate our efforts, our chances of survival are more than low. In fact I'd rate them as bloody nonexistent."

"You may be right about the CIA." Dougal shrugged. "But I don't think my chance of survival would be improved if we worked together. All the evidence points the other way."

"I have the contacts, the expertise, the—"

"It doesn't matter," Dougal continued, "that you're an ethical black hole." He leaned closer to Hanbury, savoring his newfound ability to dominate the conversation. "The problem is that you are professionally inadequate. Last weekend made that quite clear. You make contingency plans like rabbits breed, and half of them go on to form independent dynasties of their own. While fooling everyone else, you fooled yourself. You didn't even know who I was meant to be for half the time. A cut-out between you and Zelda? A hitman? A multiple scapegoat? Your man at Armageddon?"

Hatton Cross station slid along the window. The train stopped. The doors opened.

"I concede a certain loss of control." Hanbury tried the effect of a smile. "That's one reason why I need your, ah, more disciplined approach. On a different basis from before: I'm offering you full partnership. In everything. I don't just mean our present problem— I can call in a few favors, and we mustn't forget your special relationship with Zelda—"

Dougal leaped from his seat just as the rubber-rimmed doors began to slide together. One edge scraped his heel as he jumped onto the platform. The doors clunked behind him, and the train started to move.

Dougal turned and waved. Hanbury still sat in his seat with his mouth open. He did not wave back.

Dougal ambled through the western wastelands of London. There were worse ways of spending an afternoon. His mind might oblige him by producing a decision by the end of the day.

His future seemed like the weather—hot, heavy, and muggy, with the probability of thunderstorms before long. Zelda was out of bounds for the time being, while Hanbury, the CIA, and the Gravers had thoroughly hostile reasons to look for him. The police might join the hunt when Vertag's body was found with its distinctively mangled finger. Dougal had little faith in Zelda's belief that the CIA had both the inclination and the power to muzzle a British police investigation.

Moreover, the world could end at any moment, thus rendering academic not only Dougal's problems but Dougal himself as well.

History, if history continued after the apocalypse, might consider Vertag to have been one of the few enlightened thinkers of late twentieth-century civilization. In that case posterity would award Dougal the role of Judas's lieutenant: a little man, just trying to make a living, but caught up in something whose consequences he had failed to realize.

Dougal looked at himself and his predicament in the perspective of centuries, as reflected in a shop window. The window belonged to a newsagent's. He pushed open the door, jumping as a bell jangled above his head. The garlic-flavored interior was gloomy and restful.

A portly Asian was standing behind the counter. He looked up slowly from the center-spread in *Playboy*. White teeth flashed. "Sir!"

"Twenty Marlboro," said Dougal cheerfully, "and a box of matches."